Matagorda Breeze

Lyla Hopper

Joy House Publishing

Copyright © 2020 Lyla Hopper
All rights reserved.
ISBN: 978-1-7364214-0-6
Library of Congress Control Number:
2020925814

Joy House Publishing
Edited by Anika Klix

Cover photo:
Flickr user c_ambler
CC-BY-2.0

DEDICATION

To all the sailors, Marines, merchant mariners, and crusty old fishermen that I have known.

Especially you, Dad. You gave me my love for bodies of water of every size.

Acknowledgments

I could not have completed this labor of love without the help and encouragement and inspiration of many people. Certainly the most prominent of them is my husband Steven, without whom I would not have had the courage to tell this tale. My sister-in-love Hilary, best friend Tracey, and a host of other wonderful people have provided much encouragement to me in this process as well.

I must also thank my editor, Anika Klix, who may be the most patient soul in existence. Just as I am generous with commas, she is generous with her time and attention.

PROLOGUE

March 21, 2022 was a date that teachers would talk to children about in history class forever. Ruby Turner, like all the kids in her class, had heard the stories about the Cataclysm, the day when the world discovered the folly of a civilization built on oil and coal and gas that came out of the ground. Mankind had spent more than a century drilling the earth full of holes, both on land and sea. In the early 21st century, when they'd started pumping water and chemicals into the ground to force the oil out, scientists said it wasn't sustainable or safe.

They were right, as scientists often are. On March 21, 2022, at 8:32 AM, the Earth had had enough. Bedrock layers that had been geologically stable for millennia, stressed by too many wells and too much hydraulic pressure, finally gave up all that mechanical energy in one destructive heave. From Dallas, to the Red River, and north nearly to Oklahoma City, the planet shook.

In places like California, where earthquakes were common, mankind had built great buildings to sway and rock safely, with heavy dampers to keep them upright in earthquakes, but in the American heartland, they had taken no such precautions. The great skyscrapers of downtown Dallas shattered and collapsed, miles of elevated highways buckled, and sinkholes swallowed up whole blocks of homes as the ground shuddered and heaved. Hundreds of thousands of people died in the quake which lasted nearly ten minutes; millions were injured and homeless. Geologists said later that there had been a string of quakes along a line nearly a hundred miles long, creating a line of death and complete destruction over ten miles wide in places.

The rescue effort was massive, and with it came the stark realization that humankind could not continue to extract fossil fuels in that way, lest another disaster happen. The nations of the world stopped hydraulic fracturing almost at once, and within a year, no new oil or gas wells were being drilled anywhere on Earth. Within a period of time, existing wells ran dry.

It was just a matter of a few short years before the oil ran out. There was a race to develop renewable sources of energy, but the Chinese hoarded the rare metals needed for solar panels. Shipping large quantities of anything began to get very, very expensive as the supplies of oil began to dry up. Around the world, over two billion people died, cut off from vital supplies that could no longer be delivered to them. Massive governments fell in favor of more-local organization, while chaos and lawlessness thrived for three decades.

But humankind is resilient. Slowly, life began to change. The great cities of the world, unable to sustain their populations, dispersed into the open spaces and rural towns, and entirely new villages sprung up. People who had lived, depended on, and worked with the products derived from petroleum learned new ways of living. Homes and small industries worked out wind and solar power on a local scale, but problems of shipping and transportation continued.

All along coasts around the world, merchants began using sailing vessels again. Pleasure craft were used for a time, but larger vessels were needed. Eventually shipbuilders emerged using melted-down recycled plastics to make fiberglass hulls similar in shape to older, larger sailing vessels. Others began making vessels of wood and steel.

Within a generation, the earthquake of March 21, 2022 was referred to as "the Cataclysm" or "the Day." Over the decades, companies emerged regionally to operate shipping routes along the coasts, while others, with their larger ships, handled the oceanic routes. It was a dangerous job; piracy became one of the ever-present hazards of the seas, along with the weather. Hard men took the job, and few lived to old age.

Matagorda Breeze

Growing up in the remnants of the city that had once been Houston, two centuries after the Day, Ruby Turner had always wanted to sail the seas.

I

PORT OF GALVESTON

Ruby Turner walked along the docks, passing the ships tied alongside, a sea bag over her shoulder. She was redheaded, her hair in a thick braid between her shoulders. She was short and fit, striding confidently toward the vessel at the end of the pier. A tall, thin man strolled slowly beside her so she could keep up with him on her shorter legs. His dark hair was trimmed neatly above his bright blue eyes, and he too carried a sea bag. They both wore denim pants and short-sleeved cotton shirts favored by sailors in these waters, but neither wore any insignia on their collars.

Arriving at the last ship on the long dock, they set their bags down, and looked her over. The *Matagorda Breeze* was a 120-foot schooner, two-masted and gaff-rigged; her worn hull dusty and grimy. Her hull number was 26, worn and fading on the bow just below her name. The sails were loosely and messily furled on the booms, and lines were piled haphazardly on the deck. Several men lolled about on deck, none of them working. At the top of the gangplank, a surly-looking man sat atop a barrel, carefully rolling a cigarette.

Ruby looked to her companion who returned her glance with a worried face. Grim-faced and without a word, she picked up her sea bag and made her way up the gangplank. The taller sailor sighed and shouldered his own bag before following her.

"Permission to come aboard, party of two?" she said to the startled sailor, still rolling his cigarette. The man did a double-take, then looked at the two up and down, and said, "he's welcome here, if he's crazy enough, but we're not hiring no cuddlebugs, and we don't need a ship's cook, neither."

"Good thing I'm not here to be a cuddlebug, isn't it? And Colin here can tell you, I can't cook worth a damn. Here are my orders," she said, handing him a slip of paper with the Gulf Shipping Company logo.

"I'm your new captain."

II

PORT OF GALVESTON, THE PREVIOUS DAY

"You can't be serious, Commodore!" Ruby exclaimed, incredulous. She'd worked hard for her current billet, stayed out of trouble, and made sure her ship and shipmates shined in every report her Captain had made to management.

"I am, Turner. I'm pulling you from your duties as navigator on the *Costa Maya* effective immediately. I have a new assignment for you."

"But *Costa Maya* has been my ship for the last two years. I'm the second-best navigator in the fleet!" Ruby protested.

"No, you're the best navigator we've got. Old Jim up and quit yesterday when the *Gulf Winds* came in. Put his pin on my desk and walked off without another word."

"So, I'm to get the *Gulf Winds*?"

Commodore Javier Marquez, Chief of Shipping Operations for Gulf Shipping, got out of his chair and walked to the window of his office overlooking the docks. "You know how I've felt about you for the last ten years you've been with the company, Turner. You know I'm not putting you aboard our flagship, not ever. You've been a thorn in my side since the day you came on these docks asking for a deckhand job."

"So, what's my new job?" Ruby asked, suddenly nervous.

"Come here," Marquez replied, reaching into his pocket for something as she rose from her chair and stood beside him at the window.

He said, "Ruby Turner, you have bedeviled me from the first day you worked for this company. You're the only woman working at sea, anywhere that I know of and I have put up with your oddities because everything you've turned your hand to you've been damn good at. You don't make mistakes when it counts, and somehow crews accept you and there are never any problems. So, I've got a special job for you. Give me your hand."

Ruby held out her hand, and the Commodore dropped a lapel pin into it with four horizontal shining gold bars on a black field.

"... Captain?" Ruby looked up at the older man, stunned.

"Congratulations, Captain Turner. You take command of *Matagorda Breeze* tomorrow morning."

"*Matagorda Breeze*? Isn't that…" she trailed off, not sure how to continue.

"You've heard the scuttlebutt, then. Captain Nielson hung himself from the foremast the night after they left Mobile, and his navigator found him the next morning. The mate got 'em home safe, and I sent them ashore for the last week. The navigator quit, so now I'm down *three* navigators."

"But Commodore, the *Matagorda Breeze* is practically a derelict! And I've heard about that crew. That's where all the drunks and troublemakers end up."

Marquez smiled thinly. "Well, Turner, she's a perfect ship for you, isn't she? As usual, you can pick your officers from other ships, if they'll go with you. Matilda's got all the crew personnel files for you outside. Good luck, Captain. Dismissed."

"Permission to come aboard?" Ruby asked the smartly dressed sailor at the top of *Padre Island Queen*'s gangplank.

"State your name and business, ma'am?" he asked, getting a pen ready to write in his logbook.

"Ruby Turner. I'm here to see the bosun if he's around."

"He's in his cabin below. Welcome aboard. Can I show you to his cabin?"

"I know the way. Thanks."

Making her way down the narrow stairs to the cabins below deck, she knocked on the second door she came to. "Colin? You decent?"

A voice from within laughed and answered, "more decent than you, Ruby! Come in!"

Ruby Turner and Colin Sampson sat across from each other at a table at a restaurant along the Strand. On the walk over from the docks, Ruby had filled her friend in on her new assignment.

"You know he's setting you up to fail right, Ruby?" he asked.

"I know that, of course. I've never even suggested that I'd like to become a Captain, or even a mate. The Commodore jumped me over other people more qualified because he wants me to really screw it up by the numbers. That crew of misfits and ne'er-do-wells will make me lose my cool, and then he can sensibly fire me. Or that's what he's hoping. But I'm not gonna let him get me that way."

"How do you propose to do that?"

"Okay, I looked over the books and personnel files real quick, and I'm pretty sure the mate is dirty. Maybe Captain Nielson figured it out and that's why he killed himself, but Hoss Jenkins has been the one running things for a long time, and the books make little sense to me. I'll bet he's smuggling and bullied the crew into going along with it. So, the first mate has to go."

"What about the Second?" Colin asked.

"Oh, he's okay. Tom Clary is unimaginative, and boring as hell at parties, and no good at all at cards, but he can do his job well enough with someone to nudge him along. I've a mind to keep him, but I won't know until I talk to him." Before Colin could ask, Ruby continued. "The bosun is Larry Nall. Poor old guy's joints are giving out but he's hoping to work another year or two, I hear."

"Wasn't he the bosun when you first went to sea?"

"On the *Floridian*, yeah. He's a good one, just not as strong as he used to be. I trust him."

Colin began to suspect something and narrowed his eyes at his friend. "So, why are you taking me to dinner to tell me all this?"

"You want a promotion, Colin? I need a first mate, someone I can trust, and someone who leads men well. Having been a bosun for three years now, you've got what I need and you can backstop Nall when his joints are hurting him. You'll get all the usual perks plus the pay raise."

Colin looked at her wide-eyed. "Well, uhm…"

Ruby scowled in frustration and said, "Colin, seriously, are we still having to fight the fight that women bosses are a good idea? You've read your history! Before the Day, women had gotten pretty close to being equal. The years of chaos set us back, but here I am finally…"

Colin leaned forward in his seat, his hands raised, "Ruby, no! That's not it at all! I'm all for you getting a captain's billet! You're more than qualified, and with the struggles that crew has had you may be the best thing that could ever happen to them. I'm just…"

"What?"

"Not sure I'm qualified. That's a three-grade jump for me, just like it is for you. I'm sure you're ready for it, but I'm not sure I am."

"I am, Colin. I'm completely certain that you're the best First I could get, anywhere. You're loyal to your friends and crew and you're someone I trust completely. I trust you with my life, Colin. You're the best choice for this job, for a lot of reasons, but for me as the brand-new captain of that particular ship you're not just the best choice, you're the only choice."

The taller sailor took a sip of his drink before answering. "Marquez will drop a brick, you know that? I've got the *Queen* shipshape and he won't want me to leave that billet."

"Let him pitch his fit. Maybe he'll figure out that he can't outfox me this way. I'm the Captain, it's my prerogative to decide who my officers are, even if I have to promote a couple. Please tell me you'll do it, Colin. I need you. We'll tell Marquez in the morning before we go to the *Breeze*."

Colin stared at her for a moment, then said, "Okay. I'm your new First."

Ruby slumped, the tension falling off her like a wave. "Great. Let's eat, then go back to the *Queen* so you can tell 'em you're leaving and get your gear. I've got a room rented; we'll be up pretty late tonight going over the books. But first…" She pushed a lapel pin across the table to him, three gold horizontal bars on a black field. "Congratulations, soon-to-be Commander."

III

PORT OF GALVESTON

"I'm your new captain," Ruby said, carefully watching the man's reaction.

"Our new… but, Hoss said..." the sailor stammered, still sitting on the barrel.

"What, precisely, did Hoss say, sailor?" Ruby asked, setting her sea bag at her feet.

"That.. uhm... he was to be…"

"The new captain? Well, that wasn't his call to make, was it? Commodore Marquez has asked me to do it. Now, where is the mate, anyway?"

"Right here," a burly man said, squeezing his bulky body through the hatch from the lower decks. "Who's askin'?"

"Commander Jenkins, before you say anything more, read my orders," Ruby insisted, gently taking the paper from the hand of the crewman at the gangplank and holding it up for Jenkins to read. With an angry look on his face, he read the words on the form in front of him. As he read, his face got flushed and his huge fists clenched.

"But this ship was supposed to be mine! I was in line for this! I'm gonna talk to Marquez about this and…"

"Not right now you're not, Jenkins. You'll get your chance to speak to him shortly." Ruby said calmly. "Right now, all hands on deck, please."

Hoss Jenkins stared at the tiny woman standing in front of him like he would look at an insect that was bothering him. His fists clenched and unclenched several times, and he finally spoke. "Aye-aye, *Captain*." Turning to the man beside him, he bellowed, "you heard the *captain*, you idiot! All hands on deck!" The terrified sailor ran to the ship's bell and rang it sharply. Several more sailors came up unhurriedly from the lower deck, accompanied by a nervous-looking older man with a clipboard in his hands. Ruby and Colin reached into their pockets and pinned their rank pins on their collar points. Counting heads, Ruby got the twenty-one she expected to find aboard.

"This everyone?" Ruby asked Hoss Jenkins, unfazed by the big man trying to stare her down.

"Yes, *Captain*."

"Good." Raising her voice, she said, "Attention to orders: I am Captain Ruby Turner, and by order of Commodore Javier Marquez, Chief of Operations for Gulf Shipping Company, I do hereby take command of this vessel and all aboard her as of oh-nine-hundred this date. Second mate, please note in the ship's log." The man with the clipboard nodded and wrote on his clipboard.

"Your orders, *Captain*?" Jenkins asked.

"Commander Jenkins, you said you wanted to talk to Commodore Marquez. That's a good thing because he's quite interested in talking to you as well." Indicating Colin standing behind her, she went on, "Commander Sampson here will go below with you, where you will pack your gear, then be escorted to see Commodore Marquez. I'm giving you dry feet, Commander. Get off my ship."

Hoss Jenkins stood stunned for a moment, and seemed to consider saying something, then grumbling to himself, the burly man headed below with Colin right behind him.

"Anyone else dirty?" Turner asked the rest of the crew. "I know about Jenkins, and so does the Commodore. If any of you were in on it, now's your chance to speak up, and it might save your necks."

A grizzled old man leaning against the railing spoke up. "Naw, he was keepin' all the spoils for himself, missy. You know I'd not let anyone on my deck dirty themselves that way."

Ruby turned to the old man and smiled widely. "Larry, you know I had to ask. How are you, old man?"

"The joints hurt, but the men haven't fed me to the fish yet, missy. Or is it ma'am now? Hard to believe you've come this far, young lady. Captain."

"Larry, you can call me whatever you like. It's good to see you, old friend." Turning to the rest of the men, some standing with their mouths hanging open. "If any of you don't think you can take orders from a woman, you'll be given a payoff, and sent ashore with my recommendation. I'd rather have you leave honestly and find a new ship to work on, than stay and work against me. There's work to be done and we sail in a week for New Orleans."

She looked over her crew and sighed. "Sailors, I know that every one of you has had problems. Too much drinking, or fighting ashore, or problems with your captains, and that's how you ended up here. But you start today with a blank page with me, and it's up to you what you put on that page. Scuttlebutt is that I am now in charge of the worst crew on the Gulf, but I'm not buying that. I see sailors, good ones, who have been bullied by a crooked officer for too long. That stops right now. From me and my officers you will get respect and sound leadership. From you, we expect you to use your skills to serve the team and ship."

She looked at the stunned faces in front of her; they'd never heard a captain speak this way. "There's money to be made, men, bonuses and glory enough for all of us, and I have an idea how we're gonna land our fair share. Starting tomorrow, we'll get to work on that. Today, let's get things in order; you men have been traumatized long enough."

"When we're dismissed, the bosun will put you to work topside. Get things scrubbed down and clean, the lines put away, and clean this filthy deck. Once you're done here, go below and clean up your berthings and the galley. I'll be cleaning the captain's cabin, and the new first mate will be cleaning his. Second mate!"

Startled, the nervous man with the clipboard looked up. "Ma'am?"

"Do we have any paid cargo aboard?"

"No, ma'am!"

"But the cargo holds are not empty, are they?"

After a pause, Clary replied, "No, ma'am!"

"I thought they might not be. After you've got your own space squared away, I want an inventory of the ship's storage, plus whatever is in the cargo holds. Anything below that doesn't belong to one of the sailors, belongs to the ship, as of right now. Let me know what you've got, and we'll figure out what we need to keep, and what we can sell off ashore to put some money in the ship's purse."

Brightening a bit, Tom Clary straightened up taller, and said, "Aye-aye, ma'am!" Ruby and her Second locked eyes for a moment, and then she nodded. Clary would be a keeper.

At that moment, Colin came up from below, leading a furious Hoss Jenkins, who was carrying his sea bag. The mate shoved the larger man down the gangplank where two men waited to escort him to the Commodore. Watching them leave, Colin turned to his captain, and said, "he tried to go to the holds, ma'am. He didn't get there."

"Good man, Colin. Set a gangway watch, then get your cabin in order. I'll be in my cabin." Turning to the rest of the crew, she continued, "Gentlemen, you have your orders. If you need something for your own berthings, or any supplies, give your list to the Second. If you've decided you're not staying with us, pack your gear and see the First for your papers. Any other concerns come see me. At 1800, put on your best duds, and meet me at the foot of the gangplank. I'm taking us to dinner, my treat. Dismissed."

IV

PORT OF GALVESTON

Ruby opened the door to her new cabin in the aft of the ship. Stepping through, she set her sea bag on the floor then quietly closed the door for a look around.

She'd never been a superstitious person, yet the captain's cabin was unsettling, like she didn't belong here. Paperwork was still laid out on the small desk, the bed was rumpled like it had just been slept in, and pictures of Captain Evan Nielson and his family still hung on the bulkhead. The Captain was not an old man, but he'd sailed with the company for a long time. She had met him; all the senior people in the company knew each other. He had been a quiet man, with bright blonde hair and sad eyes. She'd wondered once or twice why that was, but now regretted never having sought Captain Nielson out to talk about it.

Steeling herself, she took from her pocket the key that Commodore Marquez had given her that morning; the key to the ship's safe. "We never found Evan's key ring," he'd said, "so I had a new one made from the spares. No telling what you'll find in that safe, Turner."

She went to the locker in the corner, at the head of the bunk, and squatted down on her heels to reach into the locker and open the safe. Opening it, she found a money bag with a scant few small bills and an envelope. She moved to the desk and sat down, staring at the address on the envelope, she read, *"Captain, S/V Matagorda Breeze, after June 1, 2218."*

Her hands shaking, Ruby opened the envelope and unfolded the single hand-written sheet inside.

May 25, 2218
At anchor
Somewhere southwest of Mobile, Alabama
The Gulf of Mexico

To the new Captain of the Matagorda Breeze,

By the time you read this, of course, I'm dead. As soon as I finish writing this, I'm going on deck to stand my last watch. I deliberately took the mid-watch tonight, so almost everyone aboard will be below, sleeping. For months, we've only had one person on deck during the mid-watch, keeping an eye out for pirates, but I don't think they'll get my crew tonight before the navigator comes up from belowdecks at 0400 and finds what's left of me.

I hope you have already figured out that Hoss Jenkins has been smuggling and that he had bullied me and the rest of the crew into turning a blind eye for years. So far as I know, he was the only one aboard who was in on the deal. His most recent haul was not large, so when we left Mobile, he was in a terrible mood, and he came in here and gave me no end of grief. I just can't take it anymore. I gave him most of the last of what was in the purse, just to get him away from me.

I have tried, despite all his theft and brutality, to provide for my crew. They're good men, Captain, all of them. Many of them have turned their lives around after problems on other ships, and if you nurture them, they'll serve you well, if you can get them out from under Hoss's thumb. When we left Mobile this evening, headed for Galveston, we only had four days' supplies aboard. The ship's purse is so empty that I cannot even afford to feed my crew properly, and I take full responsibility for letting Hoss starve them and work them like slaves.

I don't suppose I was ever a really good captain. I have always cared very deeply for my crew but have always been weak and easily manipulated.

But no more. When I finish here, I'll go on deck, relieve Tom and wait a bit and maybe smoke my pipe one last time, then throw my keys overboard so Hoss won't find this letter, and hang myself from the foremast. Please send my gear to my family and tell them that I love them very much. Commodore Marquez will know how to reach them.

Good luck to you, Captain, and fair winds, always, whoever you are.

Capt. Evan Nielson
S/V Matagorda Breeze

Ruby leaned back in her chair, took a deep breath, and let the tears fall. She cried for Captain Nielson, for his family, and for the pain that he went through to feel so alone in the world that he'd had to end it this way. She cried for her crew... no, *their* crew, men who had been abused and had their lives and careers stolen out from under them for years. And she cried for the fact that Evan Nielson had to sacrifice his life for Hoss Jenkins' crimes to be exposed.

After a while, she went to the tiny head in the corner of the cabin and washed her face. Then she opened the coat locker, found Nielson's sea bag, and carefully and systematically packed his belongings in the bag. Standing the bag in the corner, she returned to the desk, and painstakingly copied the words of his letter onto another sheet of paper. Then she pressed the button on the desk that would sound a buzzer in the first mate's cabin. In moments, he was knocking on the door.

"You needed me, Captain?"

Her voice still shaky, Ruby said, "Come in, Colin, and lock the door. Sit down."

Curious, the mate locked the door, and sat down across the desk from his captain and friend. She handed him the letter, and said, "Read."

As he finished reading the letter, he looked up at Ruby, her eyes still wet. "Well, there's the proof the Commodore will want, to add to what you found in the books. Are you okay, Ruby?"

"No, I'm quite sure I'm not okay. But I will be. That poor man..."

Colin rose, came part way around the desk, and opened his arms. Ruby rushed to him, wrapping her arms around his waist and crying into his chest as he held her close, without saying a word. After a few minutes, she backed away, sniffled a little, and said, "Thank you, Colin. I've made a copy. Let's witness it, and I'll take it with his things to Marquez's office. The original stays here, Colin. The crew must see it, and we need a copy in the logbook."

"I agree. Do you need me to go with you to see the Commodore?"

"No, I'll be all right. I'll only be gone a few minutes."

Ruby and Colin looked over the copy to make sure it was an exact copy, then they both initialed and dated it. Ruby locked the original in the safe and folded the copy to take with her. Shouldering Nielson's bag, she unlocked the door and said, "the ship is yours until I return, Commander."

"Aye, Captain."

Ruby returned to her ship about twenty minutes later, having passed on the bag and the copy of the letter to Commodore Marquez. Returning to her cabin, she opened the two small windows to air out the space and began unpacking her sea bag. She was just finishing making up the bunk when there was a knock on the door.

She yelled, "C'mon in, it's unlocked," thinking it was probably Colin or Larry, but the man standing in her doorway was the sailor she'd met coming up the gangplank that morning, with his cap in his hand, looking nervous.

"Come in, sailor! And do tell me your name. I've seen the personnel files, but it'll take me time to get all the names straight. Have a seat!" she encouraged him, as she moved to sit at her desk.

"Jones, ma'am. Robert Jones. And ma'am, I just wanted to come and apologize to you. We got off on the wrong foot. With that, I was wonderin' if you still wanted me aboard."

"Senior Crewman Jones, you had no reason to expect that a woman coming up the gangplank was anything but a cuddlebug. They're up and down the docks all the time, just making their living, and I can't blame them a bit for it. It was a perfectly honest mistake, and it's forgiven and forgotten. If you'll have me as your captain, I'm happy to have you aboard this ship."

The man shuffled his feet nervously. "Well, ma'am, I was thinkin' about that. What you said on deck, I mean, just before Hoss left. How you would respect us, and how we've been hurt enough already. I ain't heard anything like that on any ship I've been on. You're not like other captains, ma'am."

"No, Mr. Jones...may I call you Robert?"

"Of course, ma'am. I'd be honored."

"Robert, I'm not like other captains, it's true. I don't suppose I ever will be. I'm sure that Captain Nielson, like a lot of good captains, cared a lot for his crew. What sets me apart, I think, is that I'm not as afraid to show it, and that I make sure that people know I care about them. Some people think it makes me look weak, but I firmly believe that caring for each other, and being open about it, makes us stronger, not weaker."

"I hadn't thought of it that way, ma'am... uh… can I call you Captain Ruby, ma'am?"

Ruby smiled at the man, still so scared to be sitting in his captain's quarters like this. "Of course, Robert."

"Cap'n Ruby, the way I see it, maybe those captains did care about me. Nielson..well, maybe. It was hard to tell, what with Hoss being the way he was. We was all scared of him, no foolin'. But when you say it, like you just did...well, I feel somethin', inside, like. It makes me feel good."

He stood up and said, "Captain, I've sailed a long time on these waters, and four years on this ship. But I've always wanted to sail under a good captain, one that'd make me proud of my ship. If it's all the same to you, I'd like to stay aboard, and see if you're that captain, before I retire."

Ruby rose to come around the desk and held out her hand to shake Robert's. "Senior Crewman Robert Jones, welcome to the team. I'm glad you're here."

"Thank you, ma'am. I'll...I'll be goin' now. Work to be done, and all."

"Indeed, there is, Robert. See you at dinner. Dismissed."

V

PORT OF GALVESTON

Commander Colin Sampson looked over his new home. Besides being a crooked bully, his predecessor was a slovenly man, and hadn't been at all gentle while getting his gear together. The cabin was a mess. Colin sat his sea bag down next to the door and started cleaning up. The smelly mattress on the bunk would have to go, and he had a set of sheets of his own, once the new one arrived. He opened the small window in the side of the ship to air out the cabin.

After carrying the mattress off the ship and letting Tom Clary know he needed a new one, he got a bag from the galley and started gathering up the litter and trash in the cabin. There was a small desk, and papers were scattered atop it. He made a neat stack to go through later, then decided that the deck could use a scrub. Peering into the head, he saw that it, too, was in a terrible state. Changing into a pair of older pants and a t-shirt from his sea bag, he went to the galley for a bucket, scrub brush and some soap.

An hour later, the deck was clean and the head sparkled like new. Colin had mopped the water off the deck and wiped down all the furnishings. As he began unpacking his gear, the first sailors knocked on his door. Opening the door, two crewmen stood there, one with a frown on his face.

"Sir, I don't know why we had to do so much work on deck when we were just going to leave."

"It was your mess that was on deck, sailor, so your mess to clean up. I presume you two men want off the ship?"

"Yes, sir," the second man said. "It's just not right for a woman to be aboard ship. It's not their place. And making one the Captain, and putting her in charge? That's just wrong!"

Colin glared coldly at the man. "And what do you suppose their place is?"

"A woman's place is raisin' babies, keeping homes. I've read the histories. Just before the Catastrophe, women were able to get jobs, own property, they got treated like the men and there was constant argument over it. After the Day, everyone was paying attention to survival, and that's how it should be. It's our job as men to protect the women. It's the way it's supposed to be."

Colin sighed. "You're dead wrong, sailor, but I'm not here to argue with you. Give me your names, and I'll write up your papers and give you a chit to collect on at the Harbormaster's office."

After dismissing the two men and seeing them off the ship, he returned to his cabin to keep unpacking. He'd almost finished when there was another knock on his cabin door. The sailor standing there when he opened the door looked uncomfortable. Colin showed him in and had him sit down in a chair as he moved to sit at his desk.

"What can I do for you, sailor?"

"Well, sir, I'm not sure I can stay aboard. I mean, nothing against the Captain, she seems like a fine woman and all. No disrespect intended, sir."

"I'm sure if she were here, she would not take any, sailor. You say you're unsure? Please explain your thinking, and maybe I can help you clarify your mind."

"Well, sir, you know it's always been thought unlucky to have a woman aboard as crew. But the Captain has been with the Company a while and I ain't heard of any problems on other ships. So, I'm thinking that it might be just the opposite maybe, and she's a good-luck charm."

"That's possible, I suppose, Mr…" he trailed off, hoping the man would give his name.

"Taylor, sir. Ron Taylor."

"Mr. Taylor, it's plausible, perhaps, that Captain Turner is a lucky charm for the ships she has served. But I like to think it a little bit more likely that she is a skilled mariner who is also easy to get along with, friendly, and compassionate."

"Have you known her for long, sir?"

"For several years, Mr. Taylor. We served together on a couple of different ships and I consider her my best friend, bar none. She has been there for me in some of my low points, and I've been there for her as she's gone through the doldrums as well."

"She's pretty, too."

"She is attractive, I'll give you that. Taylor, if she were here, she'd blush and say thank you, then go on to point out that she knows what she's doing with both sextant and steel. She's worked very hard to get to where she is." They were interrupted by yet another knock on the door. Colin yelled, "Enter!" and another sailor walked in the door.

"Sorry to disturb you, sir, uh…I can come back later if…"

Colin sighed, "No, sailor, what is it?"

"I was just wanting to get my papers. We've finished on deck, and I gathered my gear and left my berthing neat. I just… well, it's wrong having a woman aboard. And it's even more wrong to make one the Captain. Women should be satisfied with their place and let the menfolk do the hard jobs."

Colin raised an eyebrow at Taylor, then looked back to the sailor standing in his doorway. "And if a woman can do the same job as a man, why on earth shouldn't she have that job sailor? Can I ask you that?"

"Uh…well, sir, it's just wrong. Men are just better than women at any job requiring strength or intelligence."

The first mate looked at the man with steel in his eyes. "Have you learned the sextant and compass, sailor?"

"Well, no, sir. I'm not too good with the maths, you know, but I'm strong, and I can pull on a line or lift a load with the best of 'em."

"So, you'll never be a Navigator, then. You should know that Captain Turner's last post was as a navigator and the Commodore considers her the best navigator in the fleet. So clearly intelligence is not the purview of men only, wouldn't you say?"

"Yeah, and that's fine for you fancy-pants officers, but she can't pull her weight on deck like the rest of us. And if the pirates come, she'll be cowering in her cabin crying for the men to protect her."

"Think so?"

"Yes, sir. That's how women are."

"Hmm. Well, clearly I'm not going to convince you, so give me your name and I'll write your papers up right quick. Mr. Taylor, keep your seat. We aren't done."

After the papers had been signed and the man was gone, Colin turned back to the sailor sitting across the desk. "Now, Mr. Taylor, where were we?"

"Uhm, sir, I…"

Colin raised an eyebrow. "Did you learn something from that little exchange, crewman?"

"I did, sir. You know, it just doesn't make any sense, what that man was saying."

"It doesn't. And attitudes like that are something that Captain Turner has dealt with for ten years, since the day she came to the docks at 18. I've heard the older sailors talk about the skinny girl who didn't even know how to hold a cutlass but worked to pull her fair share anyway. She's worked twice as hard as any man in this company to get where she is, Taylor, because of men like that one."

"I can see that. I… I guess I really admire her grit for that, sir."

"As well you should. She's got a lot of grit. She's also brave, loyal, and brilliant, and cares very deeply for the people around her. So, do you still want me to write up your papers, Mr. Taylor?"

"Uhm... no sir, I don't guess I do. I could get a job with any captain, I suppose, but... well, it sounds like Captain Turner is pretty special."

Colin smiled. "That she is." He stood up, extended his hand. "Welcome to the team, Crewman Ron Taylor."

Taylor shook his hand. "Thank you, sir."

VI

PORT OF GALVESTON

Colin was just finishing combing his hair when there was a knock on his cabin door. "You decent, Colin?"

He opened the door to find his captain there, dressed in a long, flowy skirt and comfortable pumps, and a blouse with loose sleeves and a snug bodice. A jeweled belt low on her hips held a long knife in a scabbard. "Come in, Captain. You look beautiful."

"I clean up okay. You look pretty amazing yourself, sailor." Colin was dressed in black pants with mid-shin boots, and a short-sleeved shirt that hugged his lean frame showing off muscular shoulders and arms. He was just fastening a belt around his hips and clipping a scabbard to it. He tested the draw of his cutlass slightly, then took one last look in the mirror.

"How many came to you for papers today, Colin?"

"Only three. I'll admit to being a little surprised. Jones stayed. I figured he was Jenkins' right-hand man."

"Jones came to see me, to apologize for this morning. I don't think Jenkins had a right-hand man, really. Too greedy to share the spoils, so he terrorized pretty much everyone. I'll check in with Staffing tomorrow and see who's available to fill in the gaps."

"Have you figured out what you're gonna do about a navigator, Ruby?"

Turner sighed and leaned against the doorpost. "I could do it myself, but we need another watch-stander. I'm still thinking that one over."

"I'm sure you'll come up with some idea that will annoy the Commodore. I thought steam was going to come out his ears this morning, between you accusing Jenkins of smuggling and me stepping up to be your First."

Ruby giggled. "Steam-powered Commodore...hm. Maybe we're on to a new power source there, Colin. Besides being good-looking as hell, you're also smart, too."

"Sure, and I can make a lazy deckhand reconsider his life choices without even raising my voice, too. I have many skills."

"That you do. Ready?"

"Sure, let's do this."

At the head of the gangplank, they were met by Tom Clary. "Captain, if you don't mind, I'll take gangway watch here while you and the crew are away. I can sit here and finish writing up that inventory you wanted."

"You sure, Tom? We can be sure and have someone bring you back a steak if you like."

"That'd be lovely, ma'am. No rush at all, just have someone bring it when they're headed back this way. Medium-well, please, and not too thick."

"I certainly will, Tom. Thank you. Everyone on the dock already, but us?"

"Yes, ma'am. Just waiting on the boss to arrive for the party to start."

Ruby preceded her First down the gangplank and into the midst of her crew. All of them dressed sharply, and all but one of them was carrying steel. Some were dressed simply, in clean denims and work shirts, but they had shined their shoes and cleaned up. Others were dressed more flamboyantly. Robert Jones was wearing a baggy pair of pants over boots, a loose-fitting shirt, and a broad-brimmed hat with the brim pinned up on one side. She wondered where he'd found it; she'd only seen a hat like that in old books.

Ruby walked over to the bosun who was standing next to a very tall, very broad-shouldered man, who looked quite nervous. He was the only one not carrying a cutlass. "Larry, would you introduce me to this crewman?"

"Captain, this is Crewman Tam. I'm sure you read about him in the files." The big man perked up a little, hearing his name, and smiled down at the captain.

"Yes, I have, Larry. It's good to meet you, Tam."

"Good to meet the captain, ma'am."

Tam, she recalled, had been a foundling at 13, turning up on the docks with limited skills and even less language. It was clear that he had a profound learning disability, but he was enthusiastic, and at 17, got his first job on a ship. Now, at nearly 30, Tam was strong as an ox, but other captains had reported him to be gentle as a kitten, unless threatened. Other men had tried to bully him over the years, but they only tried once; a few lumps from Tam's huge fists usually settled the matter. He had ended up on the *Matagorda Breeze* when his prior captain wrote him up several times for not doing detailed work quickly enough. The gentle giant had plainly been asked to do things that he didn't understand, then got punished for not being able to do them. She wondered what sorts of lies Hoss Jenkins had told this man in order to keep him in order, since threatening him wouldn't have worked.

"Tam, do you know why everyone calls you that?"

"Cap'n, Tam remembers mama just a little. Mama used to sing and play...like a little drum, only the drum jingled. A tam."

"A tambourine, Tam?"

"Yes'm, a tam. So, when Tam came to the docks, 'tam' was all Tam could say."

Larry chimed in. "Captain, you'll not find a man more dedicated to his ship and crewmates than our Tam, nowhere. And he's strong as they come, and not afraid of a day's hard work."

Tam was shifting from one foot to the other, hunched a little and looking nervous. Thinking fast, Ruby said, "Tam, I have a special job for you tonight. Can you help me with something?"

The man bolted fully upright, and said, "Always happy to serve the Captain, ma'am!"

"Good man. The mate knows where we are going for dinner, so he will lead the way. Would you bring up the rear with me, so no one gets lost? I'd like for the whole crew to stick together."

"Aye-aye, Captain!"

"Now, Tam," Larry said, "she's not just your Captain, she's a lady too. How do you escort a lady ashore?"

Tam thought about that for a moment, then offered his arm to Ruby. "May Tam escort the Captain, ma'am?"

"I would be honored, Tam!" she replied, slipping her hand up and into the crook of his elbow, winking over her shoulder at the bosun as they stepped away. *By the Day, he's huge,* she thought, seeing her small hand against Tam's thick arm. *He could break me in half one-handed!* The big man gently put his free hand atop hers and stood passively, waiting for the first mate to round everyone else up and head out.

Dinner was a raucous affair. Ruby had reserved a private dining room behind one of the Strand's taverns and upon arrival the staff were ready with big pitchers of ale and wine as they came in the room. Colin and a few others had declined, but when one of the waitresses, a pretty young thing with more bosom than face showing, offered a glass to Tam, the man got visibly upset and yelled "No!" at the young woman rather loudly. He began to shake. Ruby asked him what was wrong, but Larry, having heard the ruckus, came over and told her, "Tam doesn't like alcohol, Captain. He doesn't mind others drinking, but he can't stand the taste."

"Oh! Well, that's easy to solve. Tam?" Realizing she hadn't gotten his attention, she raised her voice a little, and gripped his arm gently, "Tam!"

Tam suddenly snapped to face her, somehow dragged out of his internal struggle. "Cap'n?"

"What would you like to drink, Tam? You may have whatever you want."

Tam shuffled his feet as if embarrassed. "Uhm... ma'am. Tam likes milk."

"Very well then." Turning to the startled waitress, she said, "Get this man a big pitcher of milk. And keep it coming, all he wants to drink." The young woman bobbed her head and ran to fetch the milk. Ruby suddenly realized that Tam was possibly embarrassed because of people making fun of him for liking milk instead of wine or ale.

By the time the steaks were served, Ruby had a tall mug of milk next to her glass of wine, and Tam sat nearby, grinning widely and well into his second pitcher.

VII

PORT OF GALVESTON

Senior Crewman Robert Jones had always enjoyed sleeping a little later when they were in port, but the morning after the crew of the *Matagorda Breeze* had met their new captain, he woke up about 6:30. He got ready for his day and stepped out on deck to find Ron Taylor on gangway watch.

"Anything going on this morning, Ron?"

"Quiet up here, Bob. Cap'n came out a bit ago, climbed up the mast and is just sitting up there."

Jones looked up the mast to see her sitting cross-legged, unmoving in the crow's nest far above the deck. "Hm. Mebbe she just needs some time to think. But she's got a cabin, you'd think she'd just stay holed up in there."

Larry Nall joined them on deck. "She gone up the mast, boys?" When the two crewmen told the bosun, he looked up the mast to see her sitting silently. "Sure 'nuf. I figured she would. She does that when she needs to meditate and get perspective. Best not disturb her. She'll come down when she's ready."

Bob Jones asked the older man, "Bosun, have you known our new captain long?"

"Ten years, Bob. I was the bosun on the *Floridian*, when Cap'n Leedsom and I decided to take a chance on having a girl aboard. She was a little thing then, had her hair chopped off short so she'd look more like a boy. She had a great set of eyes aloft and took to navigatin' by the stars like she was bred for it. Never minded doing the heaviest work she could, neither. She'd haul on a line with the rest of the sailors, always pulled her own weight and then some."

"And can she fight?" Taylor asked.

"You best believe it. She's so little that a cutlass was too long for her, but Cap'n Leedsom found a couple of short daggers for her in a shop in New Orleans. There was no stopping her after that. She's fast as lightning and absolutely fearless. An' she's not afraid of being in a crew full o' men, either. She'd take a berthing a little away from the others, and only once did someone try to take advantage of her. Big galoot we hired out of Pensacola, as I recall. Thought it was great that we had a cuddlebug aboard, he said. We tried to tell him she ain't no cuddlebug, but he wouldn't listen."

"He tried to slip into her berthing one night, and she rolled over and gutted him right then and there, then had to spend the rest of the night cleaning up her berthing. The people she cares about, she'll kill for without even a second thought, but she's not to be crossed, mind you. Not like that."

"She really seems super nice, Bosun," Bob said. "All that talk yesterday, about respect an' all."

"She means it, too, Bob. She's a good 'un, for sure. You don't need to mince words around her; she's heard all the guy talk and it doesn't bother her. Just respect her as your Cap'n, and she'll respect you back, be friendly-like, even a little affectionate. Those guys that left yesterday, they was all worried about women keeping their place, all that grumbling. I'm glad they're gone. Ruby Turner's place is right where she is."

Taylor said, "Bosun, you said she was affectionate. What did you mean by that? Does she… like…"

"Nothing like what you're thinking, sailor, so forget about that! But if you need a hug from a friend 'cuz your soul's at low tide, she's a good 'un for that. She gives her favors where she will, but she's not trashy about it. She's a lady, through and through. It took her a while to find that balance in her life, but she's happy being a lady, and equally happy being one of the boys." With one more glance up the mast, Larry Nall went below to start cooking breakfast

.

VIII

PORT OF GALVESTON

"Captain Ruby," as her sailors were beginning to call her, had risen with the dawn. After cleaning up and getting dressed, she went out on deck and noted with pleasure that the first mate had set a proper gangway watch overnight and climbed the rope ladder to the tiny crow's nest. Clipping a safety line to her belt, she sat on the small platform cross-legged, and looked out to the east, her hands resting comfortably on her thighs. About a half-hour later, she descended and went below, where the bosun and two others were cooking up oatmeal and bacon for breakfast.

"Cap'n, we're sorry, but we don't have a lot of supplies aboard yet," the bosun told her, and she almost cried remembering Nielson's letter, but held it together to tell Larry that it was all right and she would be arranging for supplies that day.

"Larry, brew up a pot of coffee, round up the First and Second, and bring them to my cabin. We've got work to do."

A few minutes later, the officers entered, followed by the bosun, carrying a pot of coffee and a couple of mugs. He poured his Captain a cup, then himself; the officers already had mugs in their hands.

Ruby had spread an overview chart of the Gulf out on her desk. "Gentlemen, our first scheduled run is New Orleans in less than a week. My aim is to bring this crew together as a successful group and a really obvious way to do that will be to get them making lots of money."

The bosun chuckled, "Money is a great motivator, Captain, but how do you propose to do that?"

"By delivering cargo early, as often as we can, for starters."

"Those delivery times are pretty well-defined, Captain," Tom Clary said. "How do you propose to shave time off of those runs?"

"By sailing straight across, instead of hugging the coasts."

"But, Captain, everyone knows the rigs out in the Gulf are homes for the pirates!" her Second protested.

"That's been the conventional wisdom for a long time, Tom. But a year or two ago, I started asking a few questions to myself. Where do you suppose those pirates are living, gentlemen?"

The bosun chimed in, "We've always heard they live on the old oil platforms out away from shore, missy. I mean, Captain. That's just the way things are."

"That may be, Larry, but those oil platforms are vulnerable. They're 200 years old, at least, and they're standing out there in the sea, in known locations, with salt water all around their steel hulls and hurricanes tearing through every couple of years. How many do you suppose are actually still standing?"

"Put like that, not many, probably."

"You're not buying what we've always been told, are you, ma'am?" Colin asked, speaking for the first time.

"No First, I do not buy the company line on that. It does not make any sense to me. The rigs in close to shore have all collapsed, so we know they do collapse, over time. I wouldn't think of pirates as long-game players, so maintaining some ancient oil rig for the last century and a half is not something they'd do. In the early days after the Cataclysm, maybe, but not any more. They're using something else, maybe, but they're not staying stationary. They'd be too easy to find, and too vulnerable. And that doesn't even begin to answer the question of how they keep their gang of thieves fed and supplied."

"That means, of course, that those gangs of pirates just can't be as big as we've all been led to believe, so I just don't think we have a whole lot to worry about if we sail straight across. But I have something in mind just in case we do run into them out there."

"I'm going over to Staffing shortly, and the thing I'll be looking for is men who are very good with their cutlasses, more than just strong backs. After that, I'm bringing aboard a half-dozen practice swords, and I already have a set of practice knives like my blades. Everyone aboard, including me, starts practicing their fighting skills an hour a day, starting tomorrow. Once we sail, the one-man-on-watch thing that Captain Nielson was doing at night is over; fully staffed watches around the clock."

Larry nearly snorted coffee out his nose. "You know the men won't like that, Captain."

"I don't like it much either, Larry. I need my beauty sleep! Don't worry, I'll break it to them gently. The last thing is, since we're going straight across, no more hidey-holes. We sail all night. We're done hiding."

The second mate chimed in. "That'll change our timetable quite a bit on the longer runs, ma'am."

"Indeed, it will, and we'll get some nice bonuses for faster deliveries out of it. We'll have a bit longer in port on each leg, not have to turn around quite as quickly. Everyone wins."

"It's bold," the bosun said, pouring himself more coffee.

"It is, Larry, and it's a little bit crazy, maybe. But it's time to make things better, and I think we can do it. Any other questions, gentlemen? Thank you, and remember, not a peep to the crew. Dismissed."

The bosun topped off Ruby's coffee mug and left, pot in hand. Tom followed him out, but Colin was still looking at the chart, scratching his head and apparently deep in thought.

"Something on your mind, Colin?"

"Mmm-hm. What are you going to tell Marquez when he starts asking how you and this crew of misfits are bringing in cargo faster than most?"

"Not a damn thing. I'm still the best navigator in the company, Colin, and he knows that. I was sneaky as hell on the *Costa Maya*, and we brought 'er in early with some regularity, because I found nighttime hiding places that weren't too far off the beaten path. I won't blow him away at first, just showing up a few hours early here and there. It's only 400-ish nautical miles from here to New Orleans, as the gulls fly. We'll get there in a day and a half instead of two days. He'll think I'm using my navigator's skills, and that you and I are whipping this crew into proper shape."

She rolled up the chart and tucked it into the back of her coat locker. "Want to come with me to Staffing?"

IX

PORT OF GALVESTON

Ruby and Colin walked into the staffing office, the first mate carrying a pair of wooden practice knives. Ruby asked for the files on the available sailors, and quickly looking over the dozen men's information, only saw one with anything that was an insurmountable problem. That sailor had been busted from Senior Crewman back to Crewman after getting roaring drunk and tearing up a bar on the Strand. While she admired the man's fighting spirit, she didn't understand his priorities, so dismissed him from consideration.

The two officers walked into the small waiting room where the available sailors were reading and playing cards. Several looked up seeing them enter, and one young man rose to his feet.

"Gentlemen, I'm Captain Ruby Turner of the *Matagorda Breeze*. This is my First Mate, Colin Sampson. I'm looking for three sailors, preferably ones who are good with their steel. Anyone interested?"

One older sailor, who had been slumped in the corner asleep, turned over and opened one blackened eye to peer at Ruby. "I wouldn't get on that ship with a woman captain, no way."

"You must be Mack Osborne," Ruby said. "And I suppose that it's a good thing you don't want to work with me, because I wouldn't hire you. Go back to sleeping off the drunk you got last night… *Crewman*," she finished icily. Some of the other men laughed, and Osborne *harrumphed* and rolled over.

Five sailors were out of their seats, including the young man. Ruby looked them over, and indicated they should follow her, as she turned without another word, and went outside into a fenced-off yard at the side of the building. A rack of practice swords sat under the eaves. Colin handed her the wooden swords he was carrying, then hopped up onto the fence rail to watch.

Ruby swung the wooden swords experimentally while the five sailors each went to the rack and got one for themselves. Pointing one of her blades at the biggest man, she asked, "What's your name, sailor?"

"Neal Gomez, ma'am," he replied, hefting his blade as the other four retreated to the fence with Colin.

"Crewman Gomez, show me what you've got."

The man roared suddenly and charged toward her, the hilt of his wooden sword nearly even with his shoulder on a forearm slash. Ruby raised her left blade almost vertically and turned his away from her left shoulder before it could strike. Gomez's momentum carried him past her, but he managed to stop and turn to slash again, this time on a backhand stroke. Ruby's right blade deflected his, this time, and the man backed up a step to regroup.

Watching the man move in for another slash, she raised both blades vertically, leaving herself wide open for a thrust, but the thrust never came. Gomez was strong, certainly; the impacts on her blades shook her arms and shoulders violently, but he was a one-trick pony. Finally, she ducked inside his guard, and laid her own blade neatly across the bigger man's throat. "Dead. Have a seat, Mr. Gomez."

Three other sailors each took their turn. Though all three were better than Gomez had been, only one managed to defeat Ruby. The lanky man, Senior Crewman Lew Bell, had bested her with a trick move, slipping to the side and kicking her feet out from under her. He'd looked smugly down at her, laughing in the dust, and offered his hand to help her up.

The youngest of the sailors was last. "What's your name, young man?" Ruby asked the weedy youngster, as he nervously walked toward her.

"Adamo Ramirez, ma'am."

"Crewman Ramirez, you're looking for your first ship, is that right?"

"Yes'm."

"How old are you, Ramirez?"

"Seventeen, ma'am."

"All right, Crewman, let's see what you can do."

She circled around him, watching as the point of his blade stayed low. *Too low,* she thought. "Keep your guard up, Adamo," she said, taking two quick swipes at him without making contact. The young man gulped, his Adam's apple bobbing, as he held his blade a little higher.

Ruby waited for Ramirez to charge but he didn't seem to want to. Finally, after circling around for a series of feints, Ruby charged inside his guard, putting her shoulder to his ribs and bowling him over. Straddling his ribcage on her knees, she laid her blade gently against his neck, as the other sailors laughed loudly.

She leaned down where only he could hear, and whispered, "Crewman Ramirez, you are not giving me everything you've got. I have a job for you on my ship, but you've got to give me everything. Nothing less than your best, y'hear?"

"Yes, ma'am," he whispered back, his voice shaking.

Ruby got up, then helped the youngster to his feet. "Let's try this again, Adamo. You looked like you're not used to fighting a woman. Don't think that way. Get in the moment, keep your guard up and show me some aggressiveness."

"Aye-aye, ma'am," he said, raising his sword more firmly.

Ruby took a series of easy swings at him, and he managed to parry them, only taking one clonk on the arm when he misjudged her swing. She circled around with her back to the others and grinned at him. She tossed one of her blades off to the side and made a come-hither gesture with her free hand. The young man took a swing which she parried easily. He tried again, a little harder, and Ruby winked at him and nodded.

Encouraged, Ramirez pressed his attack with a series of overhand swings, left and right, forcing Ruby to defend herself in earnest. She let him back her around the yard, and toward a corner. As she neared the corner, she ducked under a swing of his blade, and put the point of hers right up under his solar plexus in a gentle thrust. "Dead. Good job, Crewman."

Handing her blades to her first mate, she said, "Gomez, you're strong as a horse, but you're too predictable. A decent swordsman could kill you too quick. Learn some more moves." The big man walked back into the building, looking dejected.

"Bell, you're in. You're sneaky and fast, and not at all afraid to fight dirty."

Turning to the younger and more-muscular of the two remaining adults, she said, "Thompson, you've got a lot of potential, and you're strong. You're in."

"Ramirez, if we can get you over being scared of your own shadow, you'll do fine. You're in."

To the fifth man, an older, balding sailor, she said, "Mr. Jackson, you've still got a lot in you and you're a sturdy fighter. Might I suggest that you go talk to the captain of the *Costa Maya*? Tell Captain Petersen I sent you. I happen to know he's down a man or two and could use someone like you before he sails out of here for Tampa tomorrow."

"Yes, ma'am. Thank you."

Turning to the three she'd chosen, she said, "Gentlemen, get your gear and report to the *Matagorda Breeze* not later than 1400 hours. Check in with the Second and see the bosun about a berthing. I'll take care of the paperwork here."

Colin sidled up beside her as they watched the men leave the yard. "That skinny kid… Ramirez. You pushed him pretty hard."

"He needed pushing, Colin. And he'll need more pushing, and some encouragement but he'll do."

"It reminds me of how you wound me up when I first started. You chased me all around this yard with those sticks of yours. I was black and blue for a couple of weeks."

"He does remind me of you, First. You were even skinnier, though, at his age. And look how far you've come!"

"You always did have a soft spot for the tall, skinny ones, Captain."

"Oh, hush!"

X

PORT OF GALVESTON

Adamo Ramirez walked into the waiting room to retrieve his bag and left the staffing office to head down the docks. As he left, he passed Captain Turner and her first mate coming in, speaking animatedly, and laughing with each other. The captain smiled at him, and said, "See you at the *Breeze*, Mr. Ramirez."

Adamo walked alongside other ships, reading their names as he passed: *City of Beaumont*, *Gulf Winds*, *Padre Island Queen*, *Tampico Star*, *Costa Maya*. Two weeks ago, the young man had been plowing a field on his father's farm, and he realized that watching the south end of a northbound mule was not what he wanted to do for the rest of his life. He had several brothers and sisters who were happy being farmers, so that night, he discussed the matter with his father and mother, who were rather-surprisingly supportive. "You're a good boy, Adamo," his mother had said, "always kind and clever. We've known you don't belong here. There's a bigger world out there calling you. Come see us when you can, and continue being my sweet boy, wherever you go."

So Adamo had gathered a few belongings in a battered satchel and hitched a ride in a cart hauling cotton toward Galveston. Two days later, he arrived, dusty and hungry, and went to the Gulf Shipping Company docks to apply for a job. The man in the staffing office had him read a sign at a long distance to see if his eyes were good, had him lift some heavy boxes, then told Adamo that he could wait for a captain to come along to give him a chance. *And here I am, three days later heading to my first job,* he thought to himself, still scarcely believing his luck.

The three days hadn't been wasted; the staffing man had a bunch of books in the waiting room, books in which Adamo had read about sea lore and the responsibilities of his job. He still wasn't completely sure what he'd be doing, but he hoped he could learn on the job. He arrived at the gangplank to the *Matagorda Breeze*, and saw an old man at the top. He walked up to the deck, and said, "uhm…sir…"

The old-timer looked at him not unkindly, "Young 'un, save your sirs and ma'ams for the officers. I work for a living here. You can call me 'Bosun,' for now. You do know what a bosun is, right?"

"Uhm…yes, Bosun. I'm Adamo Ramirez, and I was told to report to the Second by Captain Turner."

"Mr. Ramirez, I guess you're on your first ship?"

"Yes, s….Bosun."

The grizzled bosun smiled. "Okay, then. It's traditional, when you come aboard, to ask the man on the gangway watch—that'd be me, right now— for permission to board, and if you're not a member of the crew —and you ain't yet—to say who you're there to see. So, let's try this again."

"Oh! Uhm. Permission to come aboard, to see the Second?"

"That'll do. Wait right here a moment, son." The bosun turned toward the quarterdeck, where a fair-skinned blond-haired man was seated at a table, writing. "Mr. Clary? One of the new men to see you, sir." The blond man got up from his writing and came down the steps.

"And who are you, young man?"

"Crewman Adamo Ramirez…sir." Adamo saw the bosun smile and nod behind the Second's shoulder. "Captain Turner picked me, and two others who'll be along shortly. I came straight here, sir."

"This your first ship, Mr. Ramirez?"

"Yes, sir, it is. I don't know what Captain Turner has in mind for me, but she said she had a job for me to do."

"Hm. We'll double-check with her when she gets back, but I'm betting she'll want you up in the crow's nest, if your eyes are good enough. Can you climb?" he asked, pointing at the top of the mast.

Adamo craned his neck to see the small platform at the top of the mainmast. "Oh, yes, sir, I can get up there easy, if that's what the Captain wants me to do. Or whatever else you need of me, sir."

"All right. Welcome aboard, Crewman Adamo Ramirez," Clary said, holding out his hand for the young man to shake. "Now, since the bosun is helpfully right at hand, he can get you situated in a berthing. That your gear in that old bag?"

"Yes, sir. I… don't have much," Adamo said nervously.

"I can see that. Tell you what, when you get your berthing, come see me up there," he pointed back at the table he'd been at, "and we'll see about getting you outfitted properly. Some new clothes, a shave kit, and a proper sea bag, for starters. We'll take good care of you, Adamo," he said, kindly, "you are one of us now."

"Yes, sir. Thank you, sir."

"You watch the plank a minute, Mr. Clary?" At the officer's nod, he turned to Adamo. "Come on with me, young 'un. You ever been on a ship like this before?"

"No, Bosun, I haven't."

"Okay, here's how things are laid out. Down the stairs here, in the stern of the ship, is the Captain's cabin. To port—that's the left side as you face the bow—as you move forward is the First's cabin, then mine. Amidships, the galley and the crew's head. To starboard is the Second's cabin, then the Navigator's. For'ard of that are the ship's stores and the three cargo holds. We'll take the big hatches off the top to open them to the deck for loading and unloading, but you can get to 'em along this companionway here on the port side. With me so far?"

"Yes, Bosun," Adamo said, still a little overwhelmed at being aboard a ship and being shown around like he belonged here.

"You'll be berthing in the number one hold, the farthest forward. Number one and number two holds have bunks along the sides for you men. There's only a few in number one. No bigger'n you are, it won't matter, weight-wise, where we put you, you won't affect the trim of the ship to speak of." Entering the number one hold, he took Adamo to the aft side of the hold, to a bunk near the middle of the ship.

"You want this bottom bunk here, Adamo?" he asked, showing Adamo to a small bunk, its mattress neatly rolled at the foot.

"Fine with me, Bosun."

"Okay. You'll have this locker at the foot for your gear. Do you have a lock? No? Well, ask the Second for one; keep your gear tidy and locked up. We don't often inspect to see that things are neat and shipshape, but don't get lazy and let things go to pot in here. Keeping your gear orderly is a good habit, and it lets you get what you need quickly. I'll let you get your gear squared away, then, and go back to the gangway. Once you're unpacked, go see the Second like he told you to, then you're off duty until told otherwise. Dinner will be about 1800, give or take; there'll be a bell rung in the galley when it's time for chow.

"Thank you, Bosun. Uhm…could I ask you something?"

"You're welcome. Ask away, Adamo."

"About our captain…it's not normal, having a woman captain, is it? I mean, I didn't see a whole lot of women around here since I got here three days ago."

"She's the first. And there's none like her, our Cap'n Ruby, she's a special one. You've got a winner, son, no doubt about it. Don't worry about not knowing your job, we'll teach you. Do your best for her, and she'll take good care of you."

"Thanks, Bosun. I appreciate it. I'm…really surprised she's giving me a chance. She whipped my ass in the workout yard."

"You might have noticed, she probably whipped almost everyone. She fights like a banshee, even in practice. She musta seen something in you."

"I hope so."

XI

PORT OF GALVESTON

Colin and Ruby had spent the early afternoon arranging for supply deliveries, and by the time they returned to *Matagorda Breeze*, the first deliveries of food had already arrived. The bosun was in the galley, chopping up vegetables and beef for a pot of stew.

"Once you get that cookin'," she told him," strap it down, and get everyone on deck."

"Aye, Cap'n. Are we going out?"

"Just a spin around the bay, Larry, nothing rough." The old man nodded and kept chopping.

"Colin, fly signal Papa and let everyone know to get aboard and secure so we can get underway."

"Aye-aye, Captain." He went back on deck to fly the signal flag.

A few minutes later she joined him on the quarterdeck as the men started coming out. The bosun came up from below, and said, "everyone's mustered, ma'am."

"Very well, Bosun. First, fly signal Uniform, November, Two, to request permission to leave harbor."

"Uniform, November, Two, aye, Captain. Winds are 10 knots, from the southeast, Captain."

"Sailors, a ship in harbor is safe, as we all know, but that's not what they're made for. I'd like it very much if we could rig this ship for a cruise around the bay, to see how well we can work together." Many of her crew smiled up at her, excited to be doing something for a change. "First, do you think you and this crew could take me for a short pleasure cruise?"

"Captain, I believe we can, if it's the Captain's wish."

"It is. Make it happen, Mr. Sampson."

"Aye, Captain! Bosun! Prepare to get underway, pull up the gangplank and close the rail. Prepare to cast off! Mr. Ramirez, to the crow's nest and be sure to clip a safety line to your belt! Captain, signals from the harbormaster!"

"Read them, First."

"*Matagorda Breeze*, you may proceed to sea. Fair winds to you and your crew."

"Very well, acknowledge, and secure from signals. Take her out, Mr. Sampson."

"Aye, Captain!"

In moments, the ropes holding the *Breeze* to the dock had been pulled up, and men on the dock were ready with long poles to push her away from her mooring. The first mate shouted orders, and the bosun got the sailors on lines, ready to set the mainsail. As the men on the dock pushed, the men partly lifted the gaff off the boom, opening the sail about halfway. It filled with air, and the *Breeze* slowly pulled away.

Ruby watched her crew working smoothly, the new men joining in to help as the bosun ordered them. She peered up past the sail to see young Adamo Ramirez at the top of the mast, looking out for other vessels intently. As they exited the harbor headed north, with a south-easterly wind, the mate ordered the spinnaker to be raised, and as the massive triangle of fabric caught the wind and billowed full, the *Matagorda Breeze* picked up speed.

"Any particular place in mind, Captain?"

"No, Colin, just out there a ways then we'll heave-to for a chat with the crew, and some dinner."

"Aye-aye, Captain."

Ruby pulled out her compass and took bearings off landmarks, calling them out to Tom Clary who sketched their course in grease pencil on the glass-covered chart on the chart table.

An hour out of harbor, Colin called for the sails to be doused, and set the anchor, as the ship swung around to face into the wind. Ruby sat down on the steps from the quarterdeck and called her crew around her.

"Gentlemen, yesterday when I opened the ship's safe, I found a letter addressed to me as the new captain, from Captain Nielson. I want to read the letter to you." Unfolding the letter, she started to read, her voice shaking. As she read, she felt Colin come up behind her and sit down, his hand on her shoulder. The crew listened intently as she finished, and when she looked up, there were several who looked close to tears.

"Crewmates, I don't mind telling you that I cried when I read this the first time. I cried a lot. Some of you may need to grieve for Captain Nielson, and that's okay. Come to me, or any of the officers if you want to talk, anytime. We sail for New Orleans in five days, men. I'm going to let you in on some ideas that I have. I think you need to know it and I need to be open about it, because it'll help you trust me and make us a better crew."

As she explained what she'd figured out about the Gulf oil platforms, the men all brightened. Knowing that it was unlikely that the pirates still lived there, they realized that sailing straight rather than hugging the coast would be a safer, faster passage.

"Now, that doesn't mean it's totally safe. Wherever the pirates are hiding, we may bump into them yet. And that's why, starting tomorrow, everyone will spend an hour a day in training for sword fighting. Senior Crewman Bell!"

"Captain?"

"Stand up, please, Mr. Bell. Gentlemen meet Senior Crewman Lew Bell. Lew was the only man this morning who was able to best me in sword fighting, and he did it by being sneaky and absolutely disrespectful in his fighting style. No niceties, he was in it to win it. I'm appointing him unofficial master-at-arms for the ship, and he will be leading the training that all of us, including me, will be taking. Those pirates are not in large groups; if we get attacked by one shipload of 'em, we should be able to take them."

"Now, by sailing straight, we can save a lot of time, and get some nice bonuses. But I need your help to make that happen. We're going to have round-the-clock watches every day. We'll go out every evening this week, and switch people around until we find the combinations that work. If you've got a good hand with a compass or sextant, come talk to me, and you may end up leading one of the watches, since we're still down a navigator."

There was some grumbling, but no one protested the changes.

"Bosun, would you take a couple of men with you and bring that stew up that you've had on the stove? And some of that crusty bread, I think. Let's eat, then we'll sail back to the dock."

"Aye, Captain." The old sailor pointed out a couple of men and headed below. As bowls of the hearty stew and chunks of bread were passed around, the men sat on the decks and chatted as they ate. Ruby listened to them, hearing them discussing what they'd do with the bonus money, and as they discussed among themselves which combinations of men would work best. Mentally, she was taking notes, for discussion later among her officers, but that would wait.

After dinner, and the bowls were gathered up and taken below, she called for the sail to be hoisted, and the anchor raised, and she took the helm herself to tack back toward the harbor. As the sun set, the *Matagorda Breeze* returned slowly to her dock, where the men tied her securely. As the sailors finished furling the sails, Colin came close to his captain. "You look happy, Ruby."

"I am, Colin, very much so. It felt good, giving these guys some hope, giving them something bigger to plan for."

"You know they're already crazy about you, don't you?"

"Oh, I don't know about that. All I've done is just be nice to them, for a change."

"Yeah, but you're the first person to do that in a long time."

"Check with me in six months on that, will you, Colin?" she said, as she headed below after securing the helm.

"Aye-aye, Captain. Rest well."

XII

PORT OF GALVESTON

The last week had been briskly busy as Captain Turner had worked to build her team. The work of a ship while in port, while different from a ship at sea, is no less strenuous. As the men took care of the routine matters, Ruby and her second mate looked over the leftover goods in their holds, selling most of it off, which raised enough money for a few weeks of supplies for the crew.

Adamo Ramirez spent most of a day hanging over the side of the ship on a bosun's seat, scrubbing the outside of the hull and polishing it to a beautiful shine. Someone had found some paint, and he'd turned out to have a knack for painting, having repainted the ship's name and hull number while he was working there. The bosun had appointed Tam as Ramirez's partner in this endeavor and the big man hauled ropes and handed things down to the younger sailor. After seeing their results, Ruby had praised both men at length for their hard work and led the crew in a cheer for them over dinner that evening.

The *Breeze* had gone on a few outings around the Bay, trying out different combinations of teams. The officers, after going over their notes on the crew, had decided on a "five-and-dime" watch system, dividing the day into five watches of five hours, except for the four-hour evening watch from 2200 to 0200. This required dividing the crew into three teams, each under one of the three officers, and there was much good-natured haggling around the chart table about which sailors would be on which team.

The day was sunny and fair with only a light breeze from the south. Ruby and Colin returned from the Harbormaster's office, where they had checked on the weather forecast and tides and saw that their crew was busily loading crates aboard the *Matagorda Breeze*. The doors over the holds amidships had been opened wide, and a portable boom was being used to lift the crates off the dock and set them into the hold. Tom Clary was overseeing this operation, checking the markings and counting crates as they were loaded aboard.

"Melons," Ruby groused to her first mate. "He gave us melons. Not the most glamorous cargo, but it's a good start."

Colin chuckled. "Yes, I suppose so. It'll give us a good chance to shake down and see how our gang does at sea. I'm looking forward to this little jaunt, to be quite honest."

"Oh, me too. And if we get out of here right on the morning tide tomorrow, it'll get us to New Orleans mid-afternoon Tuesday. Even for melons, that should get us a couple hundred in bonuses. We'll see what the Harbormaster there has on the dispatch board and see how quickly we can get it loaded up and move on."

The two officers walked up the gangplank where Ruby went to check in with her Second. "How's it going, Tom?"

"Just fine, ma'am. We'll have these crates all aboard in the next hour or so, then button up and be ready for tomorrow."

"Very well. When you're done, give the crew the evening off, but let them know I want everyone aboard by midnight, and everyone gets a good night's rest. My team takes the forenoon watch at 0700 tomorrow, and we sail at 0845."

"Aye-aye, Captain."—

Just before 0700 the next morning, Ruby came up from below, carrying her mug of coffee, to join the second mate standing watch on deck. "Anything to report, Tom?"

"Not a thing, ma'am. Tam and Ramirez came in just a couple of minutes after midnight. Ramirez had had a couple, and Tam got frustrated with him, so just scooped him up and carried him back here. They both went straight to bed, so they should be up by now."

"I saw them in the galley. Adamo looked a little rough, but some chow will set him right." Indeed, as they were speaking, the young sailor shuffled out on deck, blinking at the bright sunlight. He saw the captain looking at him, and grinned sheepishly, then pointed up with a questioning look.

"Good morning, Mr. Ramirez. Yes, if you can handle it, I'd like you in the crow's nest."

"Aye, Captain Ruby!" Ramirez started climbing the ropes up the mast.

Turning back to her Second, Ruby said, "Thank you, Tom. You are relieved."

"I stand relieved." He headed below to go get some breakfast.

Ruby flew the flag to let everyone know that she was preparing to get underway, and as she finished hoisting the signal, the bosun came out on deck. "Everyone's aboard, ma'am, unless someone just walked off in the last couple of minutes."

"Very well, Larry. Once you've got a hand or two, pull up the gangplank and close the rail."

"Aye, Captain."

Two hours later, as the *Matagorda Breeze* turned east just past Pelican Island and headed through the entrance to Galveston Bay, Captain Turner stood on the quarterdeck watching her crew work. The men moved efficiently around the ship, keeping eyes on the sails, now fully filled and taut in the wind. The *Breeze*'s speed slowly increased until they reached a steady 15 knots, keeping pace with the low swells of the Bay. Once they passed Point Bolivar, the captain took compass bearings off the two lighthouses on the sides of the channel, and made a mark on her chart. "Helm, make your basic course about oh-nine-five, and we'll take another sight here in a few and see if that'll get us to Louisiana or Florida."

The helmsman on watch, a Cajun named Gus Ledoux, chuckled happily. "Aye aye, Cap'n Ruby. I'm lookin' forward to seein' my home again. We've not been to N'awlins in a while. I hope you know the way!"

Ruby laughed and put her hand on the man's shoulder. "Don't worry, Gus, I think I can find it. If we miss the Mouth by a bit, we can cruise along the coast to find it."

Ruby and her team's helmsman had established a good rapport during their cruises around the Bay. The man had a great sense of humor and was eager to please his captain. He had a good eye for the sails, and could keep the deck hands on top of things in the rigging while she was taking care of charting their course without a lot of supervision. Ruby was not at all surprised that Captain Nielson had been right; these men were all skilled sailors, with not a slacker among them. They all respected her, they enjoyed working under her command, and Ruby felt completely at ease with her team.

The morning's sailing was uneventful, and as noon approached, Colin came out on deck. "Anything to report, Captain?"

We passed the remnants of a couple of oil platforms about a half-hour ago, just bits of metal sticking out of the water. You might keep watch; wouldn't want to run into one of them. But their locations are on the chart, should be no trouble. We're on course zero-nine-five, all is well. I was just about to take the noon sighting."

She reached into the drawer of the chart table and took out her sextant and watch. Taking the sighting, after some quick calculations and a glance at her book of tables, she made a small circle on the chart, joining a line of similar marks along the map. "Okay, Colin, we're about here, clipping along nicely. If the wind holds, we'll make New Orleans tomorrow afternoon. Take sights every hour. You have the conn."

"You are relieved, Captain."

Ruby went below, following several of her crew as they were replaced by the next team. The afternoon crew had prepared a lunch of sliced meats, cheese, and bread, and left it out on the galley counters for their shipmates. Ruby collected a plate and sat down next to her crew. Everyone was in good spirits with the fine weather and easy sailing during the morning. Adamo Ramirez had spent the morning in the crow's nest, and the young man was still discovering his sea legs. He and the men at the other end of the table were laughing at the way he had weaved across the deck after climbing down from the top of the mast.

As she finished her lunch, Ruby rose from her seat, and spoke to her team, "Okay, men, have a good afternoon, and we'll see you on deck at 2200 for the dog watch. Be sure and get a little rest." A chorus of good-natured grumbling followed her out of the galley as she headed to her cabin.

Ruby had spent part of the afternoon on some paperwork and napped for most of the evening. She rose about 2130, washed up, and headed to the galley for a bowl of meaty chili, courtesy of the afternoon shift. Going out on deck with her bowl in hand, she found Tom just taking a sight.

"Evening, Second."

"Good evening, Captain. Things are going well. We've kept to zero-nine-five, passed some rigs as expected, and I've marked the chart for ones that should have been there but were not observed."

"Good job, Tom. It'll be good to have updated charts. Sighted any ships?"

"Not a one, Captain. We seem to be the only thing moving out here."

"Very well, Second. I have the conn. You are relieved. Go get a bowl of chili; it's delicious."

"Aye, Captain. Have a good watch."

The wind held but for a brief period just before dawn when the ship had slowed slightly, and mid-morning, they reached the mouth of the Mississippi River. The second mate had the conn, and as they proceeded north, a small rowboat set out from Pilottown, and the watchman atop the crow's nest yelled down, "Signals! Pilottown says they're sending a pilot out to join us."

The captain was just coming on deck as Clary yelled, "Signals, very well. Reef the sails and let's let 'em catch us!" The crew hustled to pull the sails in and slow down.

"How are things, Tom?"

"Going fine, Cap'n. We missed the Mouth by about 4 miles, to the north of it. No big problem. Pilottown spotted us and is sending out a riverman to show us the way upriver."

"Very well." She looked over the chart and took out her compass for a quick bearing off of the Pilottown signal mast. Marking their position, she said, "I've got it, Tom, if you want to go below a few minutes early. There's some nice soup in the kettle."

"That'd be fine, Captain. All's well."

"Very well, Second. You are relieved."

Within minutes, they had been joined by a river pilot, a scrawny Cajun in denim coveralls and bare feet. He and Gus Ledoux immediately began speaking hurriedly in the Cajun patois. Ruby watched her helmsman conversing animatedly with the riverman, chuckling to herself. *I hadn't thought of this benefit of putting Gus on the helm,* she thought.

The rivermen knew the river like no one else, and the Company was happy to pay for their expertise. Going up and down the river was a risky business, as the silty bottom could rearrange itself between a ship's visits. This man was clearly happy to find a helmsman who had no trouble understanding his thick accent. Both men were now nodding and smiling as they spoke, and while Ruby could pick out a word or two here and there, the conversation was very hard to follow. When the riverman stopped and looked at her expectantly, Gus chimed in, "Captain, this man is Robert Lafontaine, and he'll be guiding us upriver to New Orleans."

"Good to see you again, Mr. Lafontaine."

"Ain't never seen a woman captain 'fore. But I seen you last time you's here, mebbe six, eight months 'go, on *Costa Maya*."

"Yes, I was the Navigator on that ship."

"Congrat'lations on yer new billet, ma'am."

Gus spoke up, "Captain, I've already spoken at length to Mr. Lafontaine about what we can expect on the river. We shouldn't have any surprises, though there is a sandbar developing near Venice that he'll have to guide us around."

"Excellent, gentlemen. Mr. Lafontaine, you just tell me or Gus what you need, and we'll make it happen. Would you like some coffee up here?"

"Ay, Cap'n, some coffee'd go good. Go 'head and open 'er up, an' we'n be there before midafternoon."

"You heard the man, Gus. Let's get going. I'll go fetch a pot of coffee and a mug for our guest."

As she ducked below, she heard the riverman talking to Gus again, "Your cap'n, she'n odd 'un, f'shore! Fetchin' coffee for us rivermen? Who'da thought?"

As 4 PM approached, the ship rounded the last of several hairpin curves in the river, and Lafontaine pointed and yelled out, "Yeah, lookah thah! Tol' ya we'd get ya there, Cap'n! We'n make the docks in 'bout 20 minutes, I guess."

"Outstanding work, Mr. Lafontaine. Well done," the captain said, raising signal flags herself to request permission to dock, and seeing an almost-immediate response granting permission. "Bosun!"

"Captain?" the old sailor replied from amidships.

"I think this calls for a celebration, don't you?"

"Aye, Captain, I do. A maiden voyage to be proud of!"

"Dress the ship, then, and get all hands on deck for our arrival. Dinner in the Quarter tonight!"

"Aye-aye, Captain!"

Larry Nall rang the ship's bell sharply, and bellowed, "Dress the ship, lads! Let's go!"

In minutes, everyone was on deck, and the signal flags had been strung in a colorful line from the bowsprit, to the tops of the masts, and down to the transom. The mates had joined Ruby on the quarterdeck, both smiling broadly at their Captain. Colin looked at the Company's dock near the French Quarter and saw signals being flown. "Captain, we have congratulations signals flying on *Progreso*, *City of Beaumont*, *Mississippi Mud,* and *Gulf Winds.* Harbor is signaling compliments to you, Captain, and a request that you report to the Harbormaster as soon as we dock."

"I figured Skinner would want to talk to me. Probably wondering how I did it and probably pissed as hell that we're making a big show of slipping in here a half-day early."

"Probably. But you only celebrate a first trip once, Ruby."

"It's not so much for me, Colin," she said, watching the men on deck laughing and joking as the ship closed in on the dock where men waited with lines and bumpers to secure the *Breeze.* "It's for them. These men have needed some joy for a while, and if a chewing out from Skinner is the price I have to pay to give it to them, I'll pay it every day of the week."

XIII

PORT OF NEW ORLEANS

"Captain, *Matagorda Breeze*, reporting to the Harbormaster!" Ruby said smartly as she entered the office.

The elderly harbormaster looked up from his paperwork, a sour look at his face. Ruby had to quell the urge to laugh; Jackson Skinner had always looked like he'd just finished eating a sour lemon, and when upset, as he was now, the look was more pronounced.

"Ruby Turner. I never would have thought that Marquez would have promoted you. When I got the telegram letting us know about it, I was shocked. Figured he'd send you to me for your first trip out. You wanna explain to me what that little show-off was about out there?"

"You mean, coming in all dressed, sir?"

"You know damn well what I mean, Turner!" the old man thundered, rising to his feet. "Flying all flags and making a big to-do, and you arrived hours before expected, to boot!"

Ruby put on her best innocent face. "Well, sir, you do know that as a maiden captain, it's my right to dress the ship on the first trip in. As for the schedule, well, we got some lucky breaks with the wind, is all."

"But on *Matagorda Breeze*? With that bunch of bums? How'd you get 'em out of bed this morning to get moving?"

"Oh, they weren't bad, sir. We had a good breakfast together in the galley, and the men all seem quite enthusiastic about making me happy."

"Harrumph. Well, I was expecting you just after dawn tomorrow and that you'd slip in quietly. We've got no one to unload you tonight. I guess you and that ne'er-do-well crew of yours is gonna go into the Quarter tonight?"

"We will, sir. Dinner and an early start unloading in the morning."

"I don't wanna hear from the sheriff, y'hear me, Turner? If your crew gets into any drunken brawls or gets all crazy with the cuddle bugs, you'll be leaving here without 'em come Thursday's morning tide. I'm watching you, *Captain*. Now scram!"

On the way back to her ship, she sighted the captain of *Mississippi Mud*, just coming down the gangplank of his ship. Jerry Smith ran toward her. "Ruby, it's so good to see you again! Congratulations, old friend!"

"Thanks, Jerry. I'm still a little dazed at the promotion myself."

"I knew you'd make it sooner or , back when we were on *Matamoros* together. How's your crew? I heard about Evan Nielson. Sad, that."

"We had a rough few days. Marquez gave 'em a week off when they got to Galveston, but we had some grieving to do together. But they're shaping up nicely."

"I hear you've got Tam aboard. Good man, and such a sweet soul he is."

"I do, and he's an absolute treasure. I've got a new kid aboard that has taken a shine to him and they're already thick as thieves."

"Do you have dinner plans, Ruby?"

"I don't, actually. I figured I'd take the gangway watch this evening while my crew hits the Quarter."

"Would you like some company? I could fetch over some dinner and we could sit and catch up while you're watching your ship."

Ruby thought that over. She'd been planning on some of the leftover soup from lunch for her dinner, but Jerry was fun to be around and a good friend. He'd gotten the *Mud* 18 months ago, having been promoted from the first mate's billet, and she'd love to pick the man's brain about his time as a captain. *And that's not all,* she thought to herself.

"I'd like that, Jerry. Think you can find us some good shrimp in this town?"

Smith snorted. "In this town? I can probably find us good shrimp within yelling distance. I'll bring some shrimp and pasta, maybe a big muffuletta sandwich to split if I can find one? Bottle of red?"

"That'd be great, Jerry. 1830?"

"It's a date, Captain. See you then," Jerry said as he turned and headed down the docks.

A date? Ruby thought to herself. Smiling bemusedly, Ruby headed back toward the *Breeze.*

"So that's the scoop, men," she said, after telling her assembled crew about what she'd heard from the Harbormaster. "The Harbormaster is on edge, and he doesn't want any mischief. It's time for us to make a good reputation. So here are my orders: No man goes alone, always be in a group. If one of your mates has had enough to drink, bring 'em home. No fighting! If someone gives you grief about being part of my crew, just let it go and let things be. Prove to them that you're better than that. And if you partake in the business of the cuddle bugs, you will pay them fairly, tip large, and be a gentleman about it. Treat 'em right, if you're going for that, okay?"

Several of the men murmured, "Aye, Cap'n" as they looked among themselves uncomfortably.

Ruby sighed, "Men, I know, believe me. Those ladies are doing a job, just like you, just like the dock-hands who'll unload us here tomorrow. They've got lives and families that we don't know anything about. I don't have any problem with you using their services, believe me! Just do it with respect, understand?"

"In any event, be back here by 0100. When the bars start closing up, it's time to head back to the docks. Get some rest, and we'll get up in the morning and have some chow before we start unloading. That'll be all hands so we get unloaded fast and can reload whatever they've got for us next. Tomorrow night, another relaxing evening in the Quarter then we set sail Thursday morning at first light. Everyone clear on the plans?"

A chorus of "Aye, Cap'n" answered her. "All right, then, men. You're dismissed. I have the gangway watch until someone gets back tonight to relieve me."

Colin Sampson looked up suddenly. "You, Captain?"

"Me. You go have fun. I'll keep an eye on things here, and Jerry Smith is coming by with some dinner. We'll spend some time catching up."

The mate's eyebrows shot up under his hairline. "Oh-hoh. Very well, Captain. We'll leave you to your date."

"Hush, Colin, it's not like that. I've known Jerry a long time. We were on *Matamoros* together when I started navigating. He's had *Mississippi Mud* for 18 months, and I haven't seen him in at least that long."

Colin stepped up close to his Captain and spoke quietly. "You know, Ruby, you're not fooling me. The men aren't the only ones who have needs. Maybe you do, maybe you don't, it's not for me to say. But if you do, having a friend like Captain Smith around isn't the worst thing that could happen. He's top-shelf, runs a good ship from everything I hear, and is undeniably easy on the eyes. None of our men will judge you; most of 'em would probably cheer you on. Hell, I'd stand watch for you, if you need some cabin time with someone."

Suddenly nervous, because she'd been thinking the same thing about Jerry Smith, with his broad shoulders, bright, easy smile and sandy brown hair, Ruby looked up into her best friend's eyes. "Colin, we've… we've never talked, you and me, about... us. Where we are. I just want to know that you're okay."

Colin gently took her shoulders in his hands. "Ruby, listen to me. You and I have been friends for a long, long time. I love you, you know that. But that's not how our relationship has moved. We're in a good place, and you spending some spare time with someone of good quality like

Jerry Smith doesn't bother me at all. I support you, not just as your First, but as your friend. Okay?"

"Okay. Once you're back, you can take the watch, or pick someone sober to do it. I dunno how things will go tonight. We'll see. Thanks for helping me keep my options open."

"Any time, Ruby. Have a good dinner."

XIV

PORT OF NEW ORLEANS

Ruby's crew headed into the French Quarter and the Captain had gone below to change out of her work clothes. When she returned and relieved her first mate of the gangway watch, she was dressed in a comfortable skirt and blouse. She set the chart table with a tablecloth that she found in the galley, and set out plates, flatware, and two wine glasses.

She hauled two chairs out of her cabin onto the deck and was just setting them in place at the chart table when she heard a voice coming from the dock. "Ahoy, *Breeze*!"

She leaned over the rail and saw Jerry Smith grinning up at her from the gangplank. He was dressed in dark slacks and a buttoned-up shirt. In one hand he held the handle of a large basket. "Permission to come aboard, Captain?"

"Come on up, Jerry. I've got us a place set up here."

When Smith reached the quarterdeck, she took the basket from his hand and set it on the table, then turned to hug him. "Thanks for coming, Jerry. Whatever you've got in there is bound to be better than cold soup from the forenoon watch."

"My dear Captain, I have spared no expense to bring you the finest that the Crescent City has to offer!" He pulled several small paper cartons out of the basket. "We've got a lovely shrimp scampi here, some pasta with seared bites of spicy chicken… a bottle of a lovely red wine, and…

this." He held up a small plain box. He drew it back when Ruby reached for it. "Patience, Ruby… there is a treasure worthy of any pirate in this little box. But you'll only see that after dinner. You've set us a lovely romantic place here on your chart table. Let's eat." He busied himself parceling the food out of the paper cartons and onto plates.

"I wouldn't have thought of my quarterdeck as the most romantic setting for a dinner with you, Jerry, but I'll take it. It all looks delicious!"

Dinner was relaxing and leisurely as Jerry regaled her with tales of his trips around the Gulf since taking over as captain of the *Mississippi Mud.* She asked him questions about the harbor teams in the ports and the kinds of cargo he'd been carrying lately. When they started talking about crew management, he got serious. "You known your First for long, Ruby?"

"Longer than I've known you, even. He was not only one of the best bosuns I've ever met, he's also my best friend."

Smith shifted uncomfortably. "… and he knows I'm here tonight, right? You trust him?"

"With my life. He knows, and he approves. Wait'll you meet him, he's amazing."

"Good, good. A good first mate is the biggest asset you can have when it comes to your crew. They're new with him, but they'll get to trusting him pretty quick and then things get nice and smooth and you won't have any worries. Especially with him having come up from a bosun's billet. He'll know what to do, so let him do it. I know you, Ruby; you'll be tempted to micro-manage those men. That's not your job, it's the First and the Bosun that are supposed to do that."

"I've been struggling with that. They've needed a steady hand, what with all they'd been through. I've been trying to give them that these first few weeks."

"Steady and gentle. That's the right thing to do, Ruby. Sounds like you're on top of it. I'm not surprised at all."

As they finished their meals, Ruby kept glancing at the small, plain mystery box that Jerry had brought. Smith noticed of course, and finally had mercy on her. "Full of pasta and shrimp? Okay. Open the box."

Ruby took the box and carefully opened the top to find small fried bundles of dough, with powdered sugar all over them. "Beignets! Jerry, are you trying to fatten me up? How did you have time to go all the way to Café du Monde for these?"

"Rank hath its privilege, Captain, something you might do well to remember. I remembered you liked them, so I sent one of my men for them. I told him I had a lady I'd like to impress, and he gladly ran that errand while I chased down the rest."

"Jerry! You shouldn't have. I love these things, and I was thinking it'd be tomorrow afternoon before I got any of them." She took one out and devoured it, reaching for another. "Can you believe they've been making these for 350 years? Café du Monde beignets are my whole justification for coming to New Orleans."

"Then I and my crew will see to it that you remain well-stocked with beignets, Captain. Save one for me, eh?"

Ruby took one out of the box and held it toward him, the glint in her eye daring him. Jerry raised an eyebrow and leaned forward to carefully take a bite. When she didn't pull her hand back, he smiled, and took the remaining bit of dough from between her fingers. "You know, Ruby, I think these are better this way. You can feed me beignets any time."

"Oh, really?" she said, lowering her hand to sit on top of his on the table. He turned his hand over and gently held hers.

"Yeah. Ruby, I'm having a lovely evening here with you."

"Me too. I… don't want things to get awkward later, Jerry. We've been friends a long timebut I've been thinking…" She trailed off, unsure how to proceed.

"I have too. I treasure you in so many ways, Ruby. You're amazing, and beautiful, and whatever you want of me, you shall have."

"Jerry, I want your friendship, always. That means more to me than you can know. And I appreciate the talk we've had tonight, about being a new captain. I've learned so much! But… I would like it, very much, if we could go below later, to my cabin. That is, if you want to. You're welcome to stay aboard tonight, as long as you want."

"Oh, Ruby… you have no idea how much I want to." He leaned in a little, so Ruby reciprocated, closing her eyes as his lips met hers.

Time slowed down a bit for Ruby as his kisses got hungrier. She met him with her own hunger, sighing softly.

"Ahoy, the *Breeze*!"

Flustered, the two captains pulled away from each other, Ruby blushing hotly. She looked over the rail to see her First standing there. When he saw her blush, he grinned hugely and wiggled his eyebrows at her.

"Colin!" she yelled, stomping her foot petulantly. "Get your skinny butt up here! You need to meet Captain Smith."

The mate strode up the gangplank and stepped up onto the quarterdeck. "Pleasure to meet you, Captain. Colin Sampson." The two men shook hands.

Ruby finished gathering up the plates and remnants of their meal. "Colin, you have the gangway watch. Jerry, grab the rest of this and come with me, please." She descended the steps to the deck and headed below without waiting for either man to reply. They looked at each other for a moment, and Colin shrugged.

Jerry chuckled, as he picked up the stacked plates and boxes. "Is she always like this?"

"Bossy? Yes. Flustered like this? No, this is new. A word of advice, Captain?"

"Certainly, Mr. Sampson."

"If you hurt her, make sure no one on this crew finds out, ever. There probably wouldn't be enough of you left to feed to the fish."

"Sound advice, sir. I wouldn't hurt her for anything."

"Then you'd better get below, before she starts looking for you."

XV

PORT OF NEW ORLEANS

Ruby woke slowly the next morning, feeling the warmth of her lover wrapped around her from behind. She could feel his breath against her neck as he slept.

He'd been a wonderful partner, tender and caring, and when she'd awakened in the middle of the night, he was awake, just watching her sleep, and his kisses and touch and the joyous lovemaking that followed, made her heart sing.

She reached down and took his hand, which was loosely draped over her waist. In moments, she heard his breathing change as he started to wake up. He groaned softly, then kissed the back of her neck tenderly. "G'morning."

"Morning, Jerry." She turned her head up to kiss him unhurriedly.

"I kinda wish we didn't have to get up this morning," he murmured.

"Me too, but duty calls. We've both got work to do if we're to make the tides."

"I know. You want the head first?"

"Guest's privilege, you go ahead."

Twenty minutes later, they were nearly ready for their day, and Ruby asked him, "Jerry, why don't you stay for breakfast, and meet my crew? I'm sure there will be plenty."

"You sure no one will get cross with you?"

"I don't think anyone will. My bosun is a good cook and can knock out pancakes that float on air, even in the roughest seas."

"Okay, you sold me. Let's go."

As they entered the galley together, the Second at the near end of the table looked up from his meal and bolted to his feet. "Captains on deck!" he shouted. The other men quickly rose to their feet as well.

"As you were, men!" she looked down the table at her First, who winked at her. *He put them up to that*, she thought.

As the crew resumed their places, she turned to Jerry. "Gentlemen, I want you to meet Captain Jerry Smith, of *Mississippi Mud*. Jerry, my team."

"A pleasure, gentlemen. I hear there is some good chow to be had here," he said, as the crew chuckled.

Larry Nall spoke up, "I don't know about good chow, Captain, but I'm trying. Pancakes, scrambled eggs, and crispy bacon this morning."

"That and coffee is all a sailor could want. You must be the bosun I've heard so much about."

"Larry Nall, sir. Pleasure to meet you. Help yourself."

As Jerry and Ruby sat down with plates, he looked down the table and said in a low voice, "They sure don't look like the ragtag misfits everyone has painted this crew to be."

"That's because they aren't. They're good men, Jerry, they just needed someone to respect them, is all."

After breakfast, Ruby walked her friend down the gangplank as her crew started lifting off the heavy covers over the cargo holds for unloading. At the bottom, she turned and he reached for her. She wrapped her arms around his neck as he held her hips. "You know Ruby, I wouldn't mind having that happen again. Soon."

"Me too, Jerry. I don't know what to make of this… whatever… that we've got going, but I'm not complaining."

"Where are you bound after this?"

"I don't know yet; I'll go see what's on the dispatch board here in a few. You?"

"Pensacola, on this afternoon's tide. After that, I don't really know. I could message you through the harbormasters."

"I'd like that. Maybe we can contrive it to end up in port again soon. I'll message you."

"Ruby, I…" he looked down into her eyes, helplessly at a loss for words.

"I know, Jerry. Me too. We can't make each other promises, that's not how our job works."

"It's more than that, Ruby. You're special. You're *beyond* special. I do not want to lose this."

"I don't either, Jerry. It'll work if we want it to. We can find a way."

He leaned down to kiss her gently. "You take care of yourself, honey. And take care of that crew. I think they will follow their 'Cap'n Ruby' to the ends of the earth, and not just because you have the cutest butt on the Gulf."

She laughed. "Jerry, you take care of yourself, too. We'll see each other again, soon. Fair winds to you, always, my darling man."

"And fair winds to you, love. I'll miss you."

He kissed her once more, then reluctantly headed down the docks toward his ship. She watched him for a moment, then went back up the gangplank where she was met by the bosun.

"You okay, Cap'n?"

"Yeah, Larry, I am. Something on your mind?"

"Yes, ma'am. Just wanted to let you know… as long as you're happy, the men are happy for you. We talked about it for a few minutes after breakfast. Cap'n Smith… well, he's got a good reputation. He's a fine man, no doubt about it. As long as he stays in your good graces, he's welcome on our decks any time."

"Thank you, Larry, that means a lot to me. Now, let's get these melons unloaded, and find out where we're headed next, shall we?"

XVI

PORT OF NEW ORLEANS

Walking down the docks away from the *Matagorda Breeze*, Captain Jerry Smith mused about his good fortune. He'd known Ruby for four years, and never dreamed that she would be attracted to him. She'd always been friendly, even affectionate, but Jerry had never heard any hint of her being involved with anyone and thought she either found her pleasures elsewhere, or was one of those people who didn't need that very much.

Waking up holding the passionate little fireball in his arms had been one of the biggest surprises for Jerry. Their lovemaking had been tender and slow, even joyous, like two people finding each other after being lost for a long time and discovering that they fit together perfectly.

Walking up the gangplank, he joined his crew, already stirring around on deck. His bosun, Jim Wheatley, wrote in his log, then raised his eyebrows seeing that his captain had not been aboard overnight. "Late night, Captain?" he asked.

"You could say that, Jim," he said.

"Lucky girl," Wheatley replied. "You're one of the good 'uns, Cap'n."

"No, I'm a very lucky man."

"Given the grin you were wearing walking up here, I'm guessing so. Who's the lucky lady? Anyone we know?"

"Captain Turner, from the *Matagorda Breeze*," Jerry replied, grinning even wider as Wheatley's eyes went round. "What?"

The bosun shuffled his feet nervously, "Well, Cap'n, I wouldn't want to ever tell you how to live your life. I've heard good things about Cap'n Turner, so I think it's great that you and she are close. Won't that be hard for y'all, not seeing each other all that often?"

"It will be, yes but we're both going into this with open eyes. We'll take what time we can get together, at least for now. And who knows what the tide will bring in some other day? I've known her for years, Jim, and I had no hint of how attracted we were to each other until last night. She's really, really amazing. It just kind of…happened. And I'm happy that it did."

"That's good to hear, Cap'n. I hope to get to meet her soon."

"I'm sure you will, Jim. You know, with her on the *Breeze*, I'd heard all kinds of noise about that being the ship where the bad sailors ended up, but she's got a friendly bunch over there. I know we've seen that ship on the docks and she's always looked disorderly and decrepit, but Ruby and her crew have got things really shipshape."

"Larry Nall is the bosun over there, Cap'n. He's getting on in years, but given support from the officers, he's a good 'un. I bet having it all ratty like that about killed him."

"I suspect so. I met Nall this morning; he's a hell of a cook. Anyone you know over there besides him?"

"I'd heard Tam had been sent there. I worked with him a couple years ago."

"I saw Tam, but we didn't speak. I met him, oh, five years ago, I think. Ruby says she's got a new kid aboard who really gets on with the big guy."

"Tam's not hard to get along with, usually. I bet he just adores Captain Turner."

"Yeah, she was telling me they'd gone to dinner as a crew a couple of times when she took command, and Tam was her faithful escort. Hard to picture the two of them side-by-side, though, as little as she is." Jerry chuckled to himself at that mental image.

"How small is she, Cap'n? I mean, I've heard, but I've never seen her up close."

"She's about five-one or so, barely comes up to my shoulder. And she's narrow across the shoulders, too. Tiny thing. Red hair down to her butt, in a long braid." He drifted off, thinking about his lover again, and Jim grinned at him.

"Ah, our lovesick Captain. To get to business, sir, we're just getting loaded up. We'll be out of here on time for Pensacola."

"Good job, Bosun. I'll go check the weather reports at the Harbormaster's office, and then we'll make ready to get underway."

"One more thing, Captain?" Jim said, taking his captain's arm.

"Yeah?"

"I'm glad for you, sir. Sounds like Captain Turner's a good 'un, and she'll be good to you."

"Thanks, Jim. I appreciate it. I dunno where this is going, but I'm going to be a greedy gut about it and enjoy every minute of it."

XVII

PORT OF BROWNSVILLE

In the two months that followed, the *Breeze* had made the circuit of the Gulf of Mexico hauling bananas from Honduras, cotton from Mobile, and citrus and tobacco from Florida. They consistently brought in their cargo early, and the ship's purse swelled with a share of the bonuses. The crew had galvanized into an efficient team, gaining a reputation for their skill, as well as for their conduct ashore. They took reasonable shore leaves, and the ship was always ready to carry any cargo, glamorous or not.

On one trip from Mobile to Progreso, they'd been sighted by pirates in a three-masted schooner some distance away as the *Breeze* headed southwest late in the evening. Her crew urged her to turn to fight them, but she had seen that they could easily outpace the larger pirate vessel so she had her crew trim sails, set her course close to the wind, and they sailed away from the pirates before they could make any headway.

Every port they had stopped at, she had a message from Jerry telling her where he was headed next. She replied as soon as she knew her next cargo, but they hadn't managed to connect since *Breeze*'s first time in New Orleans. When she'd arrived in Brownsville, there had been a message for her:

FROM: Mississippi Mud, Tampa, FL
TO: Capt, Matagorda Breeze, any port of call
DATE: 10 Oct 2218

See you in Brownsville. Should arrive 15 Oct. Your quarterdeck, or mine?
Miss you.
Capt. Jerry

She was expecting him to enter the harbor shortly if the dispatch board could be believed; the *Mud* had been sighted at the South Padre Island inlet about 45 minutes before. After talking with Colin she'd decided to let Jerry Smith in on the fact that she and her crew were sailing straight courses, and that's how they'd had such success.

Later that evening, Ruby Turner stood at the bottom of *Mississippi Mud*'s gangplank, a basket in her hand. The sailor at the top grinned at her. "Here to see the Captain, ma'am?"

"Yes, I am. Permission to come aboard?"

"Granted, Captain Turner. Captain Smith told me to expect you. He's in his cabin below. Uhm…"

"I think I know the way, sailor." The *Mud* was laid out almost identically to her own *Matagorda Breeze*, so she smiled at the young sailor and headed below. She knocked on Jerry's door, and when the door opened, he was grinning like a fool. He let her in, then latched the door behind her. She put down the basket of food she carried and flowed up against him for a kiss.

"I've missed you, Jerry."

"Mmm… I've missed you too, Ruby." He held her close, kissing her hungrily. When they paused for breath, he said, "now, what's this I hear about you dodging a pirate ship?"

"No big thing. My lookout spotted them about three miles out, a three-masted schooner, so we trimmed close and hauled ass."

"Be careful out there, Ruby. I'd hate for something to happen to you."

"We're careful. My crew wanted to try to take 'em out, but they were pretty far off, and I didn't want to give them time to prepare for us. We pulled in tight and boogied. The lookout was pouting for days."

"The skinny kid…Adamo?"

"Adamo, and yes, it was him. He was so proud of himself for spotting them. He's an amazing lookout now that he's got his sea legs for being up at the top."

"As long as you're okay."

"I'm a big girl, Jerry, and my crew and I can take care of ourselves if we need to." She leaned up and kissed him again. "Enough shop talk, sailor. We'll have tomorrow for that. Tonight is for us."

"Aye-aye, Captain!"

The two captains slept in the next morning.

After Jerry and Ruby had awakened and had a scratch breakfast with some of the *Mud*'s crew, they had walked hand-in-hand down the dock to the *Breeze*, and into her cabin.

"So, Ruby, I've been wondering something about you and your crew?"

"Oh?"

"Yeah. How is it that you're so often bringing home an early-delivery bonus? The *Mud*'s navigator is getting jealous and wondered out loud the other day if you were still looking for a navigator."

She grinned at her lover. "I wouldn't steal him away, Jerry. Besides, I'd probably drive him crazy since I came up from Navigator myself. Actually I've been wanting to talk to you about that. There's plenty of money to be made if you want in on the trick."

"Nothing too dangerous?"

"Not a bit. Well, no more than what we've been doing for all these years in these waters. Once I tell you, if you want me to talk to your officers, I'll be happy to."

"Okay, try me."

"It's really easy, Jerry. We sail straight across, not hugging the coast."

"But isn't that where all the pirates live, out on the platforms?"

"Jerry, you're a smart man, truly, or I wouldn't be as hot for you as I am. But you haven't put two and two together. What's happened to all the close-in rigs?"

"Most of 'em are barely sticking out of the water, just little bits of rusty metal to look out for when you're sailing near them."

"Why? Why did they fall?"

"Rust, hurricanes, weak concrete…oh," he said, suddenly understanding. "The ones farther out would be in the same shape for all the same reasons."

"Exactly. In two months of crossing back and forth, the most we've seen out of the water was about 6 feet of twisted metal. Most of them are completely submerged. We've been updating our charts as we pass near them and have time."

"And you haven't seen any pirates?"

"Just the once in a big, lumbering three-master. I don't think there are all that many pirates still out there, Jerry. But they've been a bogeyman for sailors on the Gulf for two centuries now, and we have this… cultural memory, I guess, of them being big and scary and sneaky. That may have been true 150 years ago, or even a hundred, but it's not now. So, straight across."

"That's the big secret? Straight across?"

"Well, that's not all of it. Obviously, if you're going straight across you're sailing at night, not hiding in some cove with one man on deck and everyone else sleeping. Harder for the pirates to find, when you're moving, even if there were more of them out there. We have manned watches around the clock."

"How do you do that? Four watches?"

"Five-and-dime, three teams, each led by one officer. The bosun floats around a bit since he's also our head cook. If the weather gets rough we've got extra men to bring on deck as needed, and if someone gets tired early from that, we can rearrange folks to cover."

"And your crew was willing to do that right off the bat?"

"They grumbled, sure. But when we brought that first load of melons into New Orleans over twelve hours early, and every man aboard got an extra fifty, they quit complaining. Yours will too."

"And what has the Commodore said about this?"

She stopped walking and looked up at Jerry. "Not a damn thing. He goes *harrumph* and gets all starchy when he has to fork over another bonus when we come into Galveston early, that's all."

"Hmm."

"We don't sail tight either, just a nice and relaxed pace. That way we're not making it too obvious that we've changed how we're doing things."

"I think…hm. Where are you headed next?"

"New Orleans."

"Fancy that. I'm headed the same direction. Why don't you sail with us? I'll buy the beignets," he said teasingly.

"Fine, okay, you sold me. You're a hard salesman, Captain Smith."

"Ruby, can we round up my officers so you can talk to them about this?"

"Sure. My men are loading, and don't need me for that."

"Great. Let's do this."

XVIII

OFF PORT ISABEL INLET

"Signals from *Mississippi Mud*, Captain!" Adamo shouted from his perch atop the mainmast.

Ruby looked off her stern to port and read the signal flags. *Mud* was indicating that she'd follow to port, so make sure to leave room for her. Ruby took out the single letter "C" flag and waved it over her head until she saw the signal flags being lowered on the other ship.

The first mate joined her on the quarterdeck. "Looks like good sailing weather, Captain."

"So far, so good, Colin."

"How did the *Mud*'s crew take the news?"

"They were actually excited, after I told them. I told the officers and they said they'd love to give it a try. There was some back and forth about setting up their teams, but we had that, too."

"Good. It'll be nice having another ship out there on this cruise. Not the least because most all of us can read whatever endearing signals you and Captain Smith send back and forth to each other."

Ruby blushed hotly. "Colin! If you think we haven't worked out a code, you don't know me as well as you thought you did. Besides, Jerry is a perfect gentleman; he'd never put anything sensitive out like that!"

Colin looked over her shoulder at the ship behind them, "hm… Captain, *Matagorda Breeze*, is the sexiest woman on the…"

Ruby whirled to look and saw no one signaling on the *Mud.* Colin exploded into laughter, joined by Gus Ledoux.. "Made you look, Ruby!"

"Hrmpf. I oughta have you both keel-hauled for that one, but it's too funny for that, so I won't."

Early the next morning, the ships found themselves becalmed, sails loose on the masts with not a breath of a breeze, just the slow rocking of the current inching them slowly abeam back toward the Texas coast. The two ships had drifted to within 50 feet of each other, so Larry Nall made a monkey fist on a long rope and had Tam throw it to the other ship, whereupon both crews hauled on the rope to bring the ships alongside. After making the rope fast, the *Mud*'s crew came over the rail bringing loaves of bread and a platter of cooked bacon. Jerry stepped over the rail and walked up to Ruby.

"Captain, we have bread and bacon. If you can spare the eggs and coffee, we'll have breakfast together while we wait for some wind."

Ruby looked to Larry Nall, who nodded, grinning, and went below to start cooking. Shortly, the two crews chatted over breakfast, their captains eating on the *Breeze*'s quarterdeck. "This was a good idea, Jerry. Who is the smart sailor on your crew that thought of it?"

"You wound me, Ruby. It was me."

"You were just looking for an opportunity to come over here and see me."

"Guilty as charged, but I'm glad our teams get along so well."

"Oh, me too. It'll help keep everyone out of trouble in New Orleans, too."

"My crewmen are all angels, so you must mean that my men can keep yours out of trouble, Captain Turner.'"

"Oh, hush."

An hour later, a light breeze started, so Jerry's crew went back to their ship and Ruby set sail again, closely followed by the larger schooner. The remaining journey across the Gulf was uneventful and when the *Breeze* got within sight of Pilottown the next day and she signaled for two pilots, Robert Lafontaine was in the dinghy. As his companion boarded *Breeze*, he waved up to Ruby.

"Ay, Cap'n, it's good to see you 'gain. I'm for the *Mud* today, but if you've a mug of that good coffee of your'n, I'd be sure'n give the mug to Cap'n Smith so's he can get it back to you. Or I'll bring it m'self when we get to the docks, if'n I don' have to rush to my next ship."

Ruby laughed. "Mr. Lafontaine, we can certainly manage a mug for you. Wait right here, I'll be right back." She dashed below as she heard the Cajun cackling loudly.

A few short hours later they were tied up at the dock and Lafontaine presented himself at the gangplank, empty mug in hand. He gave it to the baffled sailor at the top, saying only "Give this'n to herself 'n thank her kindly for the coffee." He turned around without another word and strolled down the docks, whistling a tune and passing a bemused Jerry Smith.

He reached the *Breeze*'s quarterdeck in a moment and chuckled as he gave Ruby a chaste kiss on the cheek. "That crazy Cajun was carrying on about you getting him coffee the whole way up the river. He gets so tickled that you don't send a man but fetch it yourself."

"Did you offer him more coffee, Jerry?"

"I did, but he had a death-grip on that mug and wouldn't take coffee from my ship. He says yours is better. I'm hurt. Don't we get our coffee from the same place?"

"We do. I'm convinced that scruffy guy is the best riverman there is and I'm always glad to get him. We never have any problems with the other rivermen, but we make good time with him on deck, get the channels just right. Plus, he and Gus get along great. He's fun to have aboard, too. He's a good guest so I don't mind fetching him coffee."

"Hey, you never bring coffee to me!"

She grabbed his shoulder and pulled him down for another kiss. "You're not a guest, dear. You're family. Isn't that right, Gus?"

"Oh, yes'm. Cap'n Jerry, you're one of our people, no doubt about it. We're happy to see you around. You make our Cap'n Ruby happy, and that makes us happy. You've got good men aboard, too. They're family too, just...in-laws, like."

"Thank you for that ringing endorsement, Mr. Ledoux," Jerry chuckled. "Ruby, the other thing that had Lafontaine all tickled was that you were leading our little convoy. He thought we'd just happened in at the same time, and I told him that we'd followed your lead all the way from Brownsville. He cackled and thought it was the most amazing thing that you were commanding not one, but *two* ships. You've got a fan in that man, Ruby."

"I'm a Robert Lafontaine fan, so the feeling is certainly mutual." Looking over toward the Harbormaster's office, she saw signals requesting that she and Jerry come see him. "Uh-oh. Wonder who stirred a wasp into Skinner's coffee."

Jerry turned and looked at the signals. "Us, probably. Guess we should go see, huh?"

"Yeah, we'd better. Tom," she called out, seeing her Second on deck supervising the unloading, "You got this?" Clary nodded and waved, so she and Jerry left the ship to see the irascible Harbormaster.

Jackson Skinner glared at the two Captains over the top of his spectacles. "Captain Smith, Miss Turner, it is known all over the Gulf that the two of you have some kind of... thing... going on, but was it necessary to flaunt it by telling the rivermen that you were sailing together?"

Jerry and Ruby exchanged glances and Jerry took the lead. "Harbormaster, it just happened that *Matagorda Breeze* and *Mississippi Mud* had similar cargo with the large shipment from Brownsville needing to be split across two ships. We were in port at the same time, so traveled together for safety from pirates. *Captain* Turner," he said pointedly, "is quite experienced on the route, with her Navigator's background, so I turned leadership of our little flotilla over to her. It was a mutual decision, and, as you know, fairly standard procedure for large shipments of this type."

"Mr. Lafontaine needed to know that we were being led by *Breeze* in order to best advise us in our course up the river, that's all. The fact that, as you mention, Captain Turner and I are in a relationship didn't affect that in any way."

"Hrrmph. Well. Nevermind then, just don't make a habit coming sailing into my harbor or my office all stem-to-stern like that. It's unprofessional."

Ruby spoke up. "Sir, do you have any specific action that either of us have done that you could claim is unprofessional, dangerous, or bad seamanship, or are you still upset at having a woman be a Captain in these waters, and being rude to me and to Captain Smith because of it?"

"Hrrmph! Out of my office, the both of you! No shenanigans in the Quarter tonight, you two. You both are out of here with the noon tide tomorrow; we've got shipments for both of you, going in opposite directions." They turned and left without another word and picked up their latest manifests from the dispatch office. Jerry was fuming, and Ruby was reserved and gloomy.

"That crusty old fart! Why, I oughta…Ruby? Are you okay, honey?"

"Yeah, I'm fine, he's always like that. He's dead set on unseating me somehow, doesn't like having a woman in a Captain's billet. He complains to Marquez about me every time I come into port here."

"Has Marquez actually acted on those complaints?"

"No… well, not yet anyway." She looked glum.

Jerry turned and held her shoulders as she looked down at her feet. "Ruby, look at me." She looked up, sadly. "You have already proven yourself. You are going to be one of the greatest captains the Company has ever had, and that's not just me saying so. Other people, from captains and harbormasters down to sailors and dock workers all hear about you and talk about you. And you're respected. Dock workers love you because you're kind to them. The harbormasters love that you're always willing to jump on a load on short notice, and you're easy to get along with at sea and in port. Your crew loves you. Hell, *my* crew loves you, too."

"Skinner is an exception, a throwback from the bad old days. Other captains are starting to change the way they treat their crews and dock hands and harbor pilots, because they see how well it's working for you. And don't forget the journey we just had. My men are over the moon about the bonus we're getting for this run, and they don't lay any of that at my feet, or my officers', but at yours. You are making a huge difference in how this business is run, Ruby. You've seen the reports; tonnage is up a few percentage points just in the two months you've had that ship. It's gonna get bigger and there's nothing at all that Skinner or anyone else can do to change that."

"Thanks, Jerry. He just…"

"I know, Ruby love. He's rude and hurtful, but hopefully the snub we both just gave him will give him something to think about." He put a finger under her chin. "Now, where would you like me to take you for dinner tonight? We'll go to Café du Monde afterward, of course."

As the captains walked back toward their ships, the *Mud*'s bosun, a muscular, stocky sailor named Jim Wheatley, came down the gangplank. "Captain Turner! A word, ma'am?"

She looked at Jerry, who shrugged. "What can I do for you, Mr. Wheatley?"

"Beggin' the captain's pardons, ma'am, sir, but the men on the *Mud* have been talking some while you two were in the Harbormaster's office.

Uhm… we know full well that we got this bonus because of you, Captain Turner. You worked out the way to sail us here that fast, and led us through the passage, and we want you to know we appreciate it. We'd like to do something for you, to thank you, ma'am."

"That's really not necessary, Mr. Wheatley, you don't have to…"

"No'm, we're all agreed up there. 'Ceptin' the Cap'n, of course, since he was with you, but we passed a cap around, took up a little collection among us to give to you as a way of sayin' thanks. Between us, it's almost a full share."

"Bosun, you do not have to do that. I and my crew will get the same nice bonus and I'll get a fair share for it, as will my ship's purse. But if you want a way to pay some respect to what I showed your officers, take that money and give it to the Lost Sailor's Fund. My crew decided a couple of weeks ago to add one more share to the divvy-up every time we get a bonus with one for the families of our brothers lost at sea."

"That's a good idea. May we give it in your name, ma'am? This time, I mean."

"If you insist, Mr. Wheatley. Thank your crewmates for the tribute. I'm honored."

"The honor's ours, ma'am. We've got a good captain, and we're glad you and he are together. It's unusual, two Captains being so close, but you're an unusual Captain, if you don't mind my sayin' so, ma'am. I'll talk to the men about making charity one of our shares, on the regular, like. It's a good idea. If the Captain approves, of course."

"Absolutely, Mr. Wheatley. Make it so."

As Wheatley headed back up the gangplank to tell his crewmates, Jerry said, "You see, Ruby? You're special, and everyone… *Everyone*, including that old fart Skinner… knows it."

XIX

PORT OF GALVESTON

Just after the New Year, Ruby and her crew had sailed into Galveston with a load of citrus from Tampa aboard. When they arrived at the dock, the dock hands immediately swarmed over the ship, hurrying to unload. The foreman told her that the commodore wanted to see her at once, so she left the ship in the hands of her crew and went to his office.

"Captain, *Matagorda Breeze*, to see the Commodore!"

"Sit down, Turner. Something has happened that you may not even know about."

"Yes, sir? Is there something wrong with my ship or crew?"

"Not at all, Captain Turner. The evening that you left Tampa, Jackson Skinner passed away. They say it was a heart attack."

"I'm sorry to hear that, sir. Mr. Skinner and I had our differences, but he was an excellent manager of that port."

"He was, and that's the problem. The Board met the following morning, and they have selected the new Harbormaster, but that person is not in New Orleans, but Mobile. You are being dispatched to pick the new Harbormaster up and take them to New Orleans to take their new post. Speed is important. The tide here peaks in the next three hours, and I want to get you out of this harbor and on your way with the tide. The staff in New Orleans are having a hard time staying organized. The foremen there are doing their best, but they just can't keep things running as smoothly as Skinner did. I don't have to tell you how important that port is to the Company."

"No, sir, I see the problem. Conveniently, we still have a cabin unoccupied."

"Right, and no one else does. I've put some supplies orders in for you, nothing you haven't ordered before, and those are being loaded right now. We don't have any cargo for you, Turner, this is a deadhead trip. Once you pick up your passenger, leave Mobile at once, as long as it's not right at low tide."

"Very well, Commodore, if I may go brief my crew?"

"Somehow, you're the fastest ship in the fleet, Turner. I still don't know how you've done it with that gang of misfits, but I can't deny the results. We need that Harbormaster in Mobile as fast as you can make that happen. When you get them to New Orleans, you'll get two days of shore leave to rest your crew as a token of the Company's thanks. Dismissed, Captain Turner."

Three hours later, the *Breeze* was passing Point Bolivar, her First Mate at the helm. "Captain, do you know who they appointed?"

"I do not, Colin. I presume they are promoting the Harbormaster in Mobile, James Henley. But he's got a family there in Mobile, so having him jump up suddenly like this doesn't make a lot of sense to me. I guess we'll find out the plan when we get there."

When they reached the docks in Mobile two afternoons later, one of the foremen, a solidly-built woman named Emma Whitaker, was standing there with a sea bag and a small trunk. Whitaker had led the load and unload gang for Ruby's ship a few times, and while the woman was occasionally somewhat terse, she was efficient, and led her crew well.

Dock hands held the ropes, not even tying off, and when Larry Nall's men lowered the gangplank, she stalked up the plank asking Larry if she'd send a man for the trunk. Confused, he did as she turned left and walked up to the quarterdeck. She held out a form to Ruby. "Captain Turner, I'm told you're taking me to New Orleans."

Ruby took the form and seeing that it was, in fact Emma Whitaker that was the new Harbormaster for New Orleans, she said, "Congratulations on your new job, Miss Whitaker. Since we don't have a navigator aboard, we have a cabin for you for our short journey. Dinner is at 1800 tonight; if you'd like, get a plate in the galley, then come to my cabin for dinner with me."

"Sounds good, Captain. How do I get to my cabin?"

"Go below, make a u-turn to starboard, and it's the second door on the right. The door is unlocked."

"Thank you, ma'am. If you don't mind?"

"Of course. You have the run of the ship, Miss Whitaker, and if you need anything, just ask any of my crew. We're here to serve you."

"Thank you." Without further talk, she turned and headed down the steps.

"A woman of few words," Colin said. "I'll bet you'll loosen her up over dinner."

"I just might, Colin. Now, let's get out of here and head for New Orleans."

"Aye-aye, Captain. Casting off now."

A few minutes after 1800, Ruby Turner and Emma Whitaker were sitting down to some dinner at Ruby's desk in her cabin. "Miss Whitaker," Ruby said, "I cannot tell you how happy I am that you're taking over in New Orleans."

"I know you and Skinner didn't get along, ma'am. His tirades are kind of legendary, so I'm guessing you are looking forward to not getting chewed out every time you go to New Orleans. No need to be shallow about it."

"Oh, but I'm not, Miss Whitaker! It's really, really nice to see a woman of your skills taking over there. We need more women at the top levels of the Company, and the Board's confidence in you speaks volumes. You've always been a great foreman on the docks, and I'm sure you'll take to your new role with the same energy and skill."

Whitaker relaxed a little, realizing she was not getting a snow job. "You think it's a big deal that they appointed a woman to the job?"

"I do. It took this Company over a hundred years to let a woman be a Captain. Now, here it is a few months later, and we have a woman as Harbormaster at one of our largest ports. Things are starting to change, Miss Whitaker, and it's past time for change. There aren't many women serving as foremen in the Company, and just the little I've worked with you, you're certainly up near the top of the list, man or woman. I'm thrilled that the Board did this, even though it's a little inconvenient for you to up and move suddenly."

Emma shrugged. "I don't have a lot of family, just a sister who lives a bit north of Mobile. We see each other once or twice a year, and we'll still be able to. So, it wasn't too inconvenient, just shocking. Oh, and call me Emma."

"Very well, Emma, I'm Ruby. Tomorrow about noon the pressure hits you, so tonight while we're sailing for New Orleans, relax. No one's expecting you to entertain them or anything; we want you to be comfortable. If there's anything any of us can do to make that happen for you, just ask."

"Thanks, Ruby. Uhm… I was thinking, just before you came into Mobile, that it might be nice to pick your brain for a while about being a woman in charge. Can we spend some time after dinner doing that?"

"Of course. I've got a bottle of wine here, and we'll open it and girl-talk for a while. For now, let's eat."

A few minutes into plates of roasted beef and vegetables, with crusty bread and butter, Emma piped up. "This is really delicious. You folks eat well on the *Breeze*."

"I put that at the feet of my bosun, Larry Nall. Besides being one of the finest sailors I've ever known, he's also an extraordinary cook. He tried to teach me a few things in the galley, back when I first met him, but he only tried once."

"Sounds like you've known him a while."

"I have. When I started with the Company a bit more than ten years ago as a deck hand, he was the bosun on the *Floridian*. He taught me an awful lot. He and Captain Leedsom were mentors to me; I owe them both a great deal."

"Mr. Nall scares me a little bit."

"Oh? Why so? He's a sweetheart."

"You don't see many old sailors, and I'm pretty sure he's one of the oldest still working. He's been a bosun longer than I've been alive. It'll feel weird being ranked higher than him."

"Don't let it get to you. He's happy for you; he said so this afternoon as we left Mobile, after you came below. When you take your plate to the galley, tell him you enjoyed the chow. You'll see, he doesn't bite. He's not the only member of my crew who's happy about your new billet, either. You might have noticed one of my helmsmen, Gus Ledoux, making cow-eyes at you when we've been in Mobile. He was remarking how nice it was going to be, having you in charge there instead of Skinner."

"Big Cajun guy, has a long drawl? Yeah, I've seen him. He's… interesting. Seems nice."

Ruby nodded. "He is. And he has family in New Orleans, so he's always happy when we go there. But we're always in a rush to get moving, because of Skinner's attitude. Now maybe he can spend a little more time with family."

"You'll get no pressure from me, Ruby. You and your crew have been good to me, and not just today. My gang and I were always happy to see you coming into harbor."

"That's good to hear. Would you care for more roast or vegetables? I'm sure there's plenty in the pot. Larry really outdid himself with this one. It's not often we have guests."

"Other than Captain Smith?" Emma said with a wicked grin.

Ruby smiled. "I don't get to see Jerry as often as I'd like. But we have a pretty good thing going, I think. He's a good man."

"I agree. He and his crew have always been really decent men, never any problems ashore. I think I'm ready for some dessert; I heard something about a peach cobbler in the galley."

"Let's go grab some and come back here and open that wine. I'll grab glasses."

After she'd poured wine and sat back down, she asked, "So, what words of wisdom can I give to a friend on this momentous evening?"

"Well, I… wait. A friend?"

"Absolutely. You've been kind to me and my crew in the past, and I'd like very much to keep in touch and be good friends. There aren't many women in the Company at all, and we're the only two at our level."

"I'd like that, Ruby. When I was told I was getting the job, some folks were a little crabby about it, including Jim Henley. He thought he should have been considered as a better candidate. So, I guess when I came aboard I was a little short and defensive. But you and your crew have been great. Nice to have… friends, that you work with."

"It is. Colin has been my best friend for years and years, along with my close friendship with Larry Nall, and Jerry and a few others. It doesn't have to harm the working relationship; I think it actually helps. I'm friendly with my crew, and they still respect me. You can have that, too, in New Orleans. Just give it time."

"How do you do that, Ruby? How do you make people look up to you so much?"

"It's not hard, really. Just be yourself, be open about what's going on, and be kind. Always kind, whenever you can. You can't always be nice, but you can always try to be kind, even when you have to lower the boom on someone."

"There's a difference?"

"There is, and I suspect you already know the difference, given your leadership style on the docks. You just might not have thought of it in that way. Something for you to think about."

"That's the big secret?"

"No big secret, really. And you're already doing a lot of that. Get in there, trust your people to do their jobs, and let them know how much you value them. Be kind, and they'll hop when you say 'frog.' You'll be fine."

Emma looked into her wine glass, swirling it around gently, thinking. "What about with the folks in New Orleans, the ones who don't work for me? The bars and restaurants, the suppliers and shops, and…" she stalled out, uncomfortable.

Ruby filled in, "And the cuddlebugs? I'll put it to you that you're going to have a better relationship with the New Orleans community than Jackson Skinner ever did. Those folks along the docks support us, feed us, supply us, entertain us, and take care of us when we're in town. Even the cuddlebugs. Those women—and a few men, let's not forget—who do that work are just as valuable to the well-being of my crew as my bosun or the shopkeeper who sells me supplies. Let all those people know that you value them, and what they do for the ships in your harbor, and you'll get along fine. Skinner was a jerk to them, *especially* the cuddlebugs."

"I… hadn't thought about them that way. I was raised different. Sleeping with someone outside of marriage just wasn't done. Paying for it, well, that was double-bad."

"Then don't do it yourself. But don't put your values on others; they already have a set of morals of their own, and it serves them well. Be kind. Realize that some of the cuddlebugs do it in order to survive, and more than a few genuinely enjoy their work, and are skilled and even artistic at it. They've got lives and families and concerns, just like you and I do."

"You feel pretty strongly about those people, don't you, Ruby?"

The captain sighed, "I do. Growing up, I had a friend whose mother was a cuddlebug. Her husband had worked himself to death way too young, and she was raising a little girl alone. You just don't know what their lives are like outside of their work, and so many people look down on them. There's no need to make their lives any worse."

"I understand. Thank you, Ruby, for making me think in new ways. I'll put it to good use, starting tomorrow when I get to New Orleans."

"You're welcome, Emma. Truly, there's nothing I really need to tell you—you know how to do the job, and you've got a good heart for people. Spend a little time on the people, and they'll happily go above and beyond for you."

Half an hour later, there was a knock on the cabin door. Ruby opened it to see Gus Ledoux standing there, with his cap in his hand. She grinned at him, her back to Emma. "What can I do for you, Gus?"

"Cap'n Ruby, uhm, Miz Whitaker, I was just out on deck a few minutes ago, and noticed that we're going to have a really beautiful sunset here in a few minutes. Miz Whitaker, I don' know if you've seen sunset from out at sea like this, but it's something special, especially the first time you see it. I…uhm…was wondering if I could show you out on deck for a look?"

Ruby turned to Emma and raised her eyebrow when she saw the woman blushing hotly. "Emma, if you'd like to go see the sunset—which, I will attest, is truly beautiful this time of year at sea—I believe Crewman Ledoux would love to escort you. Don't worry about picking up our plates and glasses, I'll take care of cleanup. Go enjoy your first night at sea."

"Ruby, I think I will. Mr. Ledoux, give me your hand, and lead the way."

XX

AT SEA, SOUTHWEST OF MOBILE

Gus led Emma Whitaker out of the Captain's cabin, and up the stairs onto the deck. Emma still didn't have her sea legs, so she stuck close to the muscular sailor leading her—at least, that's what she told herself.

Gus, for his part, was flustered and talking more than he intended to.

"…and this time of year it can look like the sun will just sizzle as it sets into the ocean. It's like…well, you'll see. Follow me." He led her forward, all the way to the bowsprit, where she hung onto the railing with both hands. Seas were light with swells of two to three feet and a fresh breeze from the southeast, filling the jib and main sail behind them.

"..and up here, it's quiet, like, y'see, because the sails stop all the wind, and…" he looked up, to see Emma looking at him intently. "But I'm talkin' too much. Are you enjoying your trip, Miz Whitaker?"

"I am. Everyone aboard has been so kind and friendly, and it almost feels like a celebration. I'm not used to being the guest of honor at the party."

"Well, maybe you should get used to it. We're all right happy for you, you know. That Mr. Skinner—he ran a good harbor, sure, but he gave our Cap'n Ruby no end of fits. We was always in a hurry to get out of Naw'lins, mostly because of him. So we see you gettin' the job as a good thing, for all of us. That's somethin' to celebrate."

"I guess you'd certainly see it that way. But call me Emma, please."

"Uh..okay, Emma. Y'can call me Gus, if y'please. So, sunsets. The sun is about five minutes from dropping below the horizon, and you see how the sky is all red and orange around it? 'Red at night, sailors' delight,' they say—it usually means good sailing weather. Those little wispy clouds up above here, they don' mean nothing, no rain'll come out of 'em. But if we look real close, just as the sun drops below the horizon, we might see a green or blue flash just for a few seconds."

"A flash?"

"Yes'm…I mean, Emma. When the sun drops below the horizon, all the red and orange light goes away, and the green and blue kinda wrap around the horizon where we can see 'em. You almost never see 'em on land because there's trees and things there to block the view. But on sea, if things are just right, it'll happen."

"Mmm… sounds lovely. While we're waiting, can I ask you a question or two?"

"Surely."

"How long have you been with the Company, Gus?"

"'Bout 8 years now, I guess. I was 22 when I started. The *Progreso* —that was before Cap'n Palmer had her—they was in Naw'lins, and needed some hefty men aboard to move cargo around. I worked there four or five years, about, then I got in a scuffle with some men who made fun o' how I talk. Ruffians like me, they said, all ended up on the *Breeze*, if'n they didn't end up in jail. I was still doin' deck-hand work when Cap'n Ruby took over the *Breeze*."

"And how did you end up as her team's helmsman?"

"Well, I can read and write, which some of the men can't, though my writin' isn't anythin' purty, y'understand, but if I slow down, I can make it readable. I'm not good with the maths that the Cap'n and the officers are, but gimme a chart and a compass, and I can at least figger things out, most o' the time, not hit any rocks or anythin'." He shrugged. "Plus, I guess, Cap'n Ruby just likes me. She's nice to work with."

"You'd do anything for her, wouldn't you, Gus?"

"Just about. An' I think any man aboard would. She's…well, she's a pretty special lady. We all love her, in our own way, I guess. And her beau, Cap'n Smith? He's a right good 'un, too. Runs a tight ship, his men are real friendly. We like to go runnin' with them when we're in port together."

Emma smiled. "One more question, Gus?"

"Uhm..sure," the helmsman stammered, suddenly nervous.

She let go of the rail and moved closer to Gus. "What about me? You've told me what the crew thinks about my job, but what about *me*? What is going on behind your big brown eyes when you look at me, Gus?"

"Ohh…you askin' the hard questions now, Emma. I see…I see the most beautiful woman on the Gulf. You're…you're just gorgeous. And you're a good person, too. That's important, to me."

"When we get to—" she paused, and tried to say it like he did, smiling, "—to Naw'lins, would you show me around? I've never been there. Your captain says there are some lovely restaurants in the old Quarter."

"Y'mean, would you like me to take you to dinner in the Quarter? Uhm…I'd be honored to, important person like you, getting a first look…"

Emma interrupted him, putting her hand in the middle of his chest, "No, Gus, not as an important person…just me. Emma."

He smiled down at her. "I'd like that." He looked over her shoulder at the sunset and pointed. "Looka there, if it's gonna flash, it'll do't here in a few seconds."

Emma turned around and leaned back against Gus as they watched the last of the red sun drop below the horizon. He carefully put his arms around her waist, his feet wide for balance on the shifting deck, and they watched in comfortable silence. Just as the sun disappeared, for a moment, there was a bright green flash. "Oh! I see it!" she said excitedly. Smiling up at him, she asked "what do the sailors think about those flashes? Are they good luck?"

He grinned, and said in a soft voice, "They sho' are for me." He leaned down a little, his eyes questioning. She nodded, and he kissed her gently.

She looked up at him shyly. "Uhm…one more thing, Gus?"

"Anything you wanna ask me, Emma."

"When do you go on watch next?"

Gus looked puzzled. "Not until tomorrow mornin', I'll be takin' us up the river to Naw'lins. Why?"

"Think we can both fit on that bed in my cabin?"

The Cajun grinned at her. "We'll figger it out."

XXI

PORT OF PROGRESO

Ruby and her crew were looking forward to a few days off, more so because they knew that the *Mississippi Mud* was in port, with a two-day overlap. Jerry had invited her and her crew to dinner ashore and the team was eagerly anticipating a good meal.

As they approached the docks, Adamo Ramirez yelled down from the crow's nest. "Captain Ruby! Harbor has seen us and asked us to come in next to the *Mud*, and for you to go to the Harbormaster at once. Harbor is flying a solid black flag, ma'am."

"Oh, no…" Staring at the flag she could barely see, she said, "that means…"

She felt Larry Nall come up behind her and put a hand on her shoulder. "You okay, Cap'n?"

"You know what that flag means, Larry. I'll get to find out who we lost shortly."

"Aye, I know. I suppose you'll be wanting the crew all together so you can tell us when you get back."

"Yeah. You all deserve to know."

When they arrived, Jerry was waiting for her at the foot of the gangplank. Ruby stepped into his arms. "Do you know what this is about, Jerry?"

"Yeah, but I'll let the Harbormaster tell you. Do you want me to come with you?"

"Could you?" she took his hand.

"Of course. Let's go."

Simón Correa welcomed the two captains into his office. "Thank you for coming in, Captain Turner. Captain Smith already knows this, but I suppose he's here to be supportive."

"That's right, Harbormaster," Jerry said.

"Okay, then. Captain Turner, I don't know how else to tell you. We've heard word from Galveston that the *Floridian* was taken by pirates."

"Oh, no…where were they?"

"They'd left New Orleans for Brownsville, and never reported in. Then this morning, Commodore Marquez received a message from the pirates, offering to sell him back the hull."

"But not the crew?"

"No, the crew… they were killed to the last man."

Stricken, Ruby clasped Jerry's hand tightly. Gathering herself, she told Correa, "Thank you for telling me this, sir. The *Floridian* was my first ship, and Captain Leedsom…" she drew a shaky breath.

"He was a good captain. I knew you and he had served together, so I wanted to tell you personally. You have aboard a former bosun from that ship, I believe?"

"Oh, Days, yes! Larry will be poleaxed by this."

"Then you'd better get out there and tell him before the dock crew does. If there's anything I can do for you or your crew, Captain, just ask. Dismissed, Captains."

Outside the Harbormaster's office, she turned and flung herself into Jerry's arms, sobbing. He wisely said nothing, just held her close, stroking her hair. After a minute or so, she wiped her eyes. "Oh, Jerry…

those pirates. I can't believe they managed to get the jump on Captain Leedsom like that. He was such a good captain!"

"I know, honey. I learned a lot from him, too. You okay?"

"I will be. Have you told your crew?"

"Yeah, I told them earlier today. We're unloaded, and off work for the day, if you'd like my gang to come over."

"I think so. Bring 'em all, and let's grieve as a family."

"Family. I like that. I'll go get 'em and see you on your deck in a few minutes."

She nodded and headed for her ship.

Her crew was gathered on deck when she arrived. She called to her First, "Colin, can you and the men stay here for a bit? The *Mud*'s crew will be joining us. Larry, you're with me, in my cabin."

"Aye, Captain."

The man followed her into her cabin. Turning to him as he latched the door, she said, "Harbormaster Correa pulled me in to tell me, before I heard about it from elsewhere, and I appreciate them doing it, because what he told me is gonna be a blow to us all."

"What happened, Cap'n? Who'd we lose?" Larry asked, nervously.

"It's the *Floridian*, Larry. Pirates got 'em. They got Captain Leedsom. They killed him and his whole crew."

Larry took in a deep breath, then started to shake. Ruby held open her arms, and the old bosun leaned in and held on, sobbing.

"It's not right, missy, it's just not! He was a good captain! He'd never let that happen!"

"They must have surprised him, somehow, Larry. Nothing else makes any sense."

"Aye, they'd have to. That crew was never lazy, never had a problem with 'em. Jack ran a tight ship," he said, dissolving into more shuddering sobs.

Some minutes later, Ruby asked, "Are you gonna be okay, Larry?"

"Yeah, I think so. I've lost friends before, in this business. But this one is a surprise."

"I know, it is to me, too. You ready to go tell the others?"

"Aye, Captain. Let's do this."

When they got back on deck, they found Jerry and his crew just arriving. The crew joined hers on deck, while the officers came up to the quarterdeck. "Gentlemen," she began, "I have terrible news. You've seen the black flag flying, and most of you know what that means; we lost a ship. I went and talked to the Harbormaster, and he told us that the *Floridian* was taken by pirates. Commodore Marquez received word this morning that the pirates have asked for a ransom for the ship. The crew… none of them survived the attack. They were attacked on their way from New Orleans to Brownsville."

"Some of you served with Captain Leedsom, or had other friends on that ship, I know. It hurts to lose a friend. If you need someone to talk to, come to me or Jerry, or any of the officers. We've all got today and tomorrow off, so let's take the time to work through the feelings. Captain Leedsom was a mentor to me, he was my first Captain, and this comes as quite a shock. That's all I've got, men. I wish I knew more, but that's all the information I have. Jerry, are we still on for dinner tonight?"

"We are, if you like, Captain. I understand if anyone doesn't want to go."

Larry spoke up, "Captains, I'll stay here. Since we're right next to the *Mud*, I can take gangway watch on both ships, if you don't mind. I'll set a chair on the dock where I can see 'em both. I need some time alone to think."

"Thank you, Larry. I'm sure someone will be coming home early tonight, to relieve you for each ship," Ruby said.

"It's no bother, Captain. Keeping watch will give me some time to work it out in my head. Raise a toast to Cap'n Leedsom for me tonight, will you?"

"I will, Larry."

Dinner was a much quieter affair than originally planned. During the meal, Ruby rose to her feet, tapping her glass for attention. "Gentlemen, a toast with whatever you drink." Both crews rose to their feet. She raised her glass. "To Captain Jack Leedsom and his crew: colleagues and friends. They lived on the sea, and they died on the sea. May their souls find safe harbor."

XXII

PORT OF PROGRESO

Later that night, snuggled up next to Jerry in her cabin, Ruby was troubled. "I still just don't understand how Jack Leedsom could have gotten caught like that. The hiding places back in those swamps off the Mouth are hard to find. The pirates would have had to spend a lot of time watching ships come and go, and…"

"And what? They've got the time to do that," Jerry answered.

"But something about this just doesn't add up to me, Jerry. They'd have had to come in force and catch them while they were anchored while not too many men were up and about. In the dark swamps, you could slip right up on someone, sure, and an inattentive lookout…maybe. It'd take a good dose of luck, too. A pirate would almost have to know… oh, no…" she trailed off.

"What?" Jerry asked.

"If it was a dark night, with little to no moonlight like tonight, the pirates would almost have to know where they'd be. Otherwise, they'd pass right by *Floridian* in the dark and not see them."

"Sure, on a moonless night you can pass within a couple hundred yards of a ship with no lights and not see 'em, everyone knows that."

"Don't you see? Somehow, the pirates knew where they'd be. The moon was new just four nights ago so those swamps would have been as dark as the inside of a sack. If the pirates were just trolling around looking, they'd never have spotted a ship in any of the hiding places. Someone, somewhere, has to be tipping them off!"

"I don't know, Ruby. That sounds pretty far-fetched. But supposing you're right, why would someone do it? Profit?"

"Probably getting cut in on the spoils, sure. Seems like that'd be the obvious answer. But how to find out who? There's gotta be a pattern to it, somehow, Jerry. Certain areas, or something. Hm. The Harbormasters get all the reports of pirate activity to share with the navigators. I wonder how far back Correa has them?"

"He and his wife are both detail fiends, and he's been on this billet for six or seven years, I think. We could see tomorrow. I'll go with you and ask for the files."

"Thanks, honey. I might be chasing shadows, but…"

"But nothing, sweetheart. It makes sense to you, so it's worth digging into. I'm happy to help."

The next morning after breakfast, the two captains walked over to the Harbormaster's office, and asked his assistant, who was also his wife, for the files on pirate activity.

"How far back do you want?" Señora Correa asked. "I've got folders for each year, for the last seven years. "Señor Correa insists that we should keep them."

"Señor Correa is a smart man. I'll take 'em all," Ruby said.

They took the stack of folders to a table nearby, and started leafing through the reports: taken ships, reports of pirate sightings, and more-rarely, the times when pirates were defeated in battle. Ruby got some paper and pencils and they started taking notes. There weren't that many reports to read, so in a couple of hours they handed the folders back to Señora Correa, and thanked her. In Ruby's cabin they rolled out a chart of the gulf and started marking it up with colored pencils.

An hour later, Jerry leaned back, and said, "You see it, don't you?"

"Yes. Yes, I do. Be careful, Jerry. You get high-value cargo and passengers more often than I do."

"We'll be careful. Fortunately, we sail straight through almost all the time now, and we have full watches around the clock, like you do. What are you going to do with this?"

"Not much I can do, really. If we can figure out who the leak is, who's tipping them off, and how, maybe…but we really can't sort that out from what we have here. It could be anyone who's got access to the dispatch boards, anywhere in the Gulf."

"Let me know if you figure things out? I'll tell you if I think of something."

"Just not over telegram. We wouldn't want to tip them off."

"Of course."

The next day, both ships loaded up and sailed off. Ruby stared at the chart late into the night after they'd left port.

The next morning, she rose with the dawn, spent some time on the bowsprit clearing her mind, then headed below to breakfast. As she finished eating, she told Larry to round up the officers and come to her cabin.

Shortly, the three men came into her cabin, and Colin latched the door.

"Gentlemen, what I tell you in here goes nowhere today, not to the men, not to anyone. Are we clear?"

At the nods from all three men, she continued. "Harbormasters get the reports of all piracy incidents against the company, plus any others that we or the company find out about. On this chart, I've marked the locations of all the piracy incidents in the Gulf in the last seven years. Red stars indicate a ship capture's approximate location, black indicates an evasion or a sighting, green is a battle where the pirates lost. Beside the star is the local time of the day of the incident, as best we know. As you can see, they're mostly clustered up in two distinct groups."

Indeed, the map had the most stars along a stretch of coast between Port Eads and Marsh Island, Louisiana, and another smaller cluster in the Bay of Campeche between Tampico and Merida, Mexico. Isolated marks were elsewhere on the map.

The two officers peered closely at the chart as the bosun considered it from farther away, sipping his coffee. Ruby went on, "We all know what happens in a ship capture. The crew gets killed or ransomed, the cargo stolen, and the passengers and hull ransomed since hulls are arguably the most valuable part of the equation. The heavy fiberglass hulls, like the *Breeze*'s, are especially valuable because they are difficult to make and increasingly rare. But if you look at these, not as isolated events but as common threads, there are patterns."

"More than two-thirds of the red-star and all the green-star events happened when the ship was carrying high-value cargo or passengers. All of the green and almost all of the black-star events happened either late in the day, as the ship was hunting for a place to hide for the night, or just in the morning, as they were leaving some quiet anchorage, and the red-star incidents seem to be happening at night, based on the last reported locations of the ships."

Colin looked up suddenly. "But that would mean…"

"Exactly, First. It means that someone is tipping them off, somewhere. It may be an inside job, or a supplier, I don't know yet. But given our doctrine that we change the hidey-holes from time to time, the pirates have to be getting lucky, even in the times when they know something valuable is coming through."

"Jerry and I were talking about it the night we found out about the *Floridian*, and we went and got all the piracy reports from the Harbormaster. There are patterns. No two hits on the same night, ever, and after each red-star event, there's a break of a few months before we start seeing them again. So, one gang of pirates, perhaps two that collaborate, not many ships, and when they make a haul, they don't run again for a while. That speaks to me of good planning and coordination, too."

"Now, Tom, what happens when a ship meets up with pirates, and wins the day?"

"Doesn't happen often, Captain, but when it does, they kill the pirates, tow the hull the pirates were using back in, or assign a prize crew, and the crew gets a fat bonus."

"Exactly. Now, all five of the green-star events on this part of the Gulf here reported killing between six and ten pirates. A group that small would have to get lucky to get the jump on a larger ship's crew, and when they've tried, they tend to lose."

The first mate looked at his captain, his eyes wide. "Captain, it sounds like you have a plan. And I don't know if I'm gonna like it."

"You know me too well, Colin. We'll get a high-value cargo at some point, and we'll go back to the old way, or appear to go back to it, and find us a hiding spot somewhere along here," she pointed at the swamps along the Louisiana coast, "and not be too obvious about it, but not be super-sneaky, either. See if we can catch us some pirates."

Larry piped up, "But, Cap'n, there's no telling when we'll get a load where the timing works out."

"No, there's not, and we may have to try this stunt a couple of times before we get caught. We'll just have to be patient. It'll come."

XXIII

GULF OF MEXICO

The *Matagorda Breeze* had left Tampico the day before with two passengers aboard. The wealthy businessman, a rotund Mexican named Emilio Gomez, was bringing crates of smoked fish with him to New Orleans, planning to discuss regular sales of the fish to restaurants and suppliers in the area. He'd planned on a working vacation and brought his wife, Imelda, along for the trip. The two passengers were very genial and seemed to enjoy their first night at sea.

When they had left Tampico, the weather reports from farther south showed a storm brewing in the Bay of Campeche. The weather to the north was very stable, so Ruby's crew had been keeping a weather eye out; a tropical storm could spin up and rush north with not much notice. In the nine months she'd led the *Breeze*'s team, they'd been in a few soft gales, but never anything heavier. The previous season, there had been a big storm farther east, off the Florida coast, but no Company ships were lost, having stayed close to shore and finding safe harbor.

This one had Ruby worried; they were out in the open water, and therefore vulnerable. The winds had picked up a bit from the southeast and were nearing 20 knots. The sea was choppy, with four and five-foot waves.

"Colin," she said as the watch was about to change, "I'm going to put us on storm watch. This thing's coming, and I think it'll miss us to the west, but it's going to be a wild ride. Let's cut farther east, see if we can get away from it. Head northeast, as much as you can. Should be able to stay on starboard tack for a while, but if the waves get much higher, we'll turn and run north."

"Sounds like a good plan, Captain," he said, turning the ship's wheel to alter course. "That wind is coming on strong."

After passing the order around that no one was to go on deck without a safety line and seeing to the lines strung across the deck, she knocked on her passengers' cabin. Imelda Gomez answered, looking a little queasy from the ship's motion. She spoke English slowly. "Can I help you, Capitána?"

"Señora Gomez, I'd like to speak to you and your husband for a moment, if you don't mind."

"Please, come in."

Emilio Gomez was sitting at the small desk, writing, and looked up from his work. "Capitána, we certainly did not expect this sort of a trip. I gather the winds have gotten worse."

"They have Señor. I've put the ship on storm watch, and we've set our course farther to the east to try to get away from the storm. We're safe enough for now, and we'll know more by tomorrow morning. I came to ask you and your wife to please secure your belongings as much as you're able to and to please not go out on deck. It'll be much safer for you down here. The galley will be serving sandwiches and other simple food for dinner since we can't cook in this rough sea."

"Thank you for telling us, Capitána. We will obey your orders, and we will pray for our safe passage in the capable hands of you and your crew. I'm not sure that Señora Gomez will be able to eat, her stomach is so upset." Indeed, the woman had sat down on the bed, her eyes closed.

"Señora, the bosun will have soda crackers in the galley. I've found that when the seas are roughthey can help keep your stomach settled. Nibble them slowly, and sip slightly-warm water. It does help to keep your eyes closed, so you don't see things moving around."

Imelda Gomez nodded, and said only, "Gracias, Capitána."

"Thank you, Capitána, for your concern and advice. I will take care of my wife and get her the crackers if she wants them."

"Señor, I and my officers are here to help. Please let anyone know if you need assistance in any way," she said, turning toward the door.

"I will, Capitána. Thank you."

Throughout the evening, as the storm grew, her crew worked short shifts on deck. The rain started about nightfall, and after an hour at a time on deck, everyone was coming below exhausted and soaked to the skin, even with their rain gear on, from the blowing spray. At about midnight, the ship heeling to and fro with the waves hitting the *Breeze* broadside, she decided to turn north and run with the wind.

The wind was at gale force, with 20-foot waves pummeling the ship. Reefing the mainsail almost to nothing, she ordered the jib set to propel them forward into the dark and keep them pointed north. With no stars out, they had no idea where they were or where they were headed, so she set a watch on the bow to keep an eye out for derelict oil rigs or other ships.

The long night was exhausting for everyone aboard, but as the sun dawned on the horizon, they could see that the sky was clearing to the northeast. The storm had turned west and struck the coast, blowing itself out in the shallower water. Around them, the swells were getting smaller.

Ruby came out on deck to relieve her Second Mate, who was manning the helm. "Isn't that a beautiful sight, Tom?" she said, pointing at the sun peeking over the horizon.

"Aye, Captain, it is. That was a rough blow, but I think we missed the worst of it."

"I think so, too. Let's go back to standard watches. You and your gang get below and get some rest. You are relieved, once you tell Señor Gomez that it's safe on deck now."

"Thank you, Captain. Have a good watch."

A few minutes later, the portly man came up through the hatch, a mug of coffee in his hand. Joining her on the quarterdeck as Ruby turned the helm over to Gus Ledoux, he said, "Truly, it is a beautiful morning, Capitána!"

"That it is, señor. I trust Señora Gomez is recovering from the rough ride."

"She is much better now, yes. Your suggestion of soda crackers and water was most helpful. She has declined breakfast and is resting in our cabin. Capitána, I was wondering if last night's storm will delay us arriving in New Orleans?"

"We were a little ahead of where I had expected to be when the storm hit us, so I expect we're still more or less on time. I'll know more when the sun gets higher, and I can get a fix on our position."

Gomez looked stunned. "You mean, you don't know where we are?"

She showed him to the chart table. "The problem with navigating by the sun and stars, señor, is that you have to be able to see them. Our last confirmed position was here," she pointed at a marked spot, "but after that, cloud cover kept us from taking sights. We went northeast for a while, then north, but with no landmarks to see, it's hard to say precisely where we are. Here in about twenty minutes, when the sun is above the horizon, I'll be able to tell. We should be somewhere about…here," tracing a circle southeast of New Orleans.

"And it's not dangerous to not know exactly where you are?"

"Not a bit, really. We have a lookout for anything in or on the water, and he's also looking to see if he sees land. Otherwise, there's nothing around us but water. Have no fear, señor. We'll get you there. If we're farther east than I think we are, we sail northwest to get back to New Orleans."

"I had no idea, Capitána. I had thought these voyages were planned with utmost precision. But it truly is an art, is it not?"

"I suppose you could say that Señor. There is some skill involved, and we learn the waters we sail in, but there are always surprises."

"Thank you for your explanation, Capitána. I look forward to hearing updated information from you."

"My pleasure, señor." The man went back down the steps leading below, beaming broadly at his new knowledge. Ruby turned to her helmsman, who was chuckling.

"What?" she asked him.

"You're so patient, Cap'n. That poor guy thought we were totally lost, didn't he?"

"I think so. He seems happier now, though. You need more coffee, Gus? I'm gonna get another mug, to brace me for the heavy work of un-losing us."

"No, thank you, Captain. I'm good. Enjoy your coffee."

XXIV

TAMPA

The *Breeze* was in Tampa for a couple of days, having brought a load of shrimp and salted fish from New Orleans. More and more, the *Matagorda Breeze* was given time-sensitive loads, and perishables were shipped farther than they had been in many years. They had just managed to leave New Orleans a couple of days before a tropical storm stirred up the Gulf, coming ashore between New Orleans and Mobile. Ruby and her crew were waiting a couple of days to give the backside of the storm time to clear the coast, and then they were headed to Progreso with a load of citrus.

A block away from the Company docks was a street of restaurants, bars, and shops. Adamo Ramirez and Tam were walking down the street, looking for a place to get something to drink. It was a hot day. Earlier in the morning, they had taken a carriage ride over to the mouth of the bay, to see the ruins of the large bridge, fallen since shortly after the Day.

Adamo enjoyed being with the gentle giant. Ever since they'd worked together to clean the hull of the ship his first week on the job, Adamo had grown close to the man. He saw in Tam a gentle soul, caring and kind. He didn't just like working with Tam; they had become fast friends. Being able to help his friend understand the world around him better made Adamo feel good. Between that and his skilled eyes atop the mast, he felt a strong sense of responsibility and purpose, and Adamo found that it suited him, in a way that being a farm boy never had.

The captain had talked to Ramirez about their friendship a couple of weeks after their first cruise and pointed out that Tam was calmer and easier to work with since he felt safe when the two of them were together.

"Captain, it's like having a kid brother, sort of, only one that's a lot bigger'n me. I want to keep Tam safe and happy. He's really a caring man, just doesn't know how to express himself sometimes," he'd said.

A day or two later, Adamo asked the bosun if he could move his gear to be in the empty berthing above Tam's. Tam occasionally had nightmares and would wake up yelling incoherently, so he had a berth farther from his crewmates, at the bow-end of the number one hold. Tam was overjoyed at Adamo's move, happy to have company nearby. Adamo hoped that he could be close by to help calm the big man when those dreams came.

It had become a matter of routine when Adamo went ashore that Tam accompanied him, and this day, they'd enjoyed learning a little bit of history of the former metropolis. Peering in the open door of a bar, Adamo said, "Tam, how about we get something cold to drink here?"

"Okay, Adamo. Can Tam have milk?"

"Sure thing, Tam," the young sailor said, walking in the door, Tam right behind him.

The room was nothing fancy, just a barroom with tables all around and a long bar across the back of the room. A piano sat silent against one wall. A few customers were drinking and talking. The bartender looked over at them and said, "Can I help you?"

"Tam's thirsty," Tam said.

Looking at Adamo, the bartender said, "Who's 'Tam'?"

"His name is Tam, and we're both thirsty."

Eyeing Tam warily, the bartender asked, "Does he always talk like that? He doesn't look drunk, is he just dumb or what?"

"He's not drunk. I'd like…"

"Look, we're not looking for any trouble here," the barkeep said, "we don't need some big dumb ox getting sauced up and trashing the place."

"He is not a dumb ox! And we're not here to trash anything!"

"Look, I'm not serving him! And if you're gonna argue with me, I ain't serving you, neither!"

"TAM IS THIRSTY!" Tam bellowed suddenly.

Adamo turned to Tam to calm his friend down, but a couple of the bartender's men were already reaching for his arms. The burly men grabbed Tam, while a third had his arms around Adamo from behind. Adamo ducked suddenly to try to get away, but the man had him firmly held. Adamo kicked behind him, connecting with the man's shin, and they both went down in a heap. Tam pulled and struggled, his eyes wide, but the two men had him contained as the bartender came around to join in the fray.

Adamo and the man who had grabbed him rolled around on the floor a moment, then Adamo rolled away and hopped to his feet. The bartender was on top of him in a second, shoving him toward the door as the third man joined his mates to hold Tam. As he reeled out the door and fell into the dust at the side of the street, Adamo thought, *the captain will not like this!*

Ruby was strolling along the street, window-shopping for a gift for Jerry, when she heard a commotion from down the street. Looking up, she sighted Adamo Ramirez getting shoved out a doorway into the street, where he fell in the dust. He sprang to his feet, looking back the way he had come, as three large men were shoving Tam out the door. He had a panicked look on his face, his eyes wide as he struggled against the men holding him. Ruby sprinted for the scene as a wiry bald man with a handlebar mustache came out of the bar's door.

"What happened here, Adamo?" she asked as she stopped near him.

"Cap'n! Me an' Tam were just coming by for something to drink. We'd gone to see the ruins of the big bridge, and it's pretty warm out."

The wiry man spoke up. "I'll not have the big dummy getting drunk and tearing up my bar. When I told him I wasn't serving him, he got loud and yelled that he wanted a drink."

Ruby glared icily at the man and spoke in a low, dangerous voice. "Sir, first of all, I wasn't even speaking to you; your input was neither required nor requested. Secondly, this man isn't a dummy of any sort; he is a valued member of my crew. Thirdly, there wasn't any need to manhandle Crewman Tam and Crewman Ramirez, if you'd just been civil to them."

Ignoring the spluttering man, she walked over to Tam and put her hand on his arm gently. Tam was shaking, still struggling to get loose from the men holding his arms. "Tam? Tam! Can you hear me?"

The giant looked down at her, "Cap'n? The man tried to hurt Adamo. Is Tam in trouble?"

"No, Tam, not at all. Adamo is fine, see?" she drew the young sailor closer. "See, Tam? He's not hurt, just dusty. You did very good to protect him, Tam. Can you tell me what happened?"

"Tam and Adamo were thirsty, Captain. Adamo led Tam here, but the man yelled and then tried to hurt Adamo."

"It's all right, Tam. Stay here with Adamo a moment, and we'll get you something to drink." She glared at the men holding him. "Gentlemen, you can unhand my crewman this instant, or we will be pressing assault charges against you." The men looked to their boss, who nodded, and they released Tam, who immediately moved closer to Adamo and his captain.

"Adamo," she asked, "is anyone else from the *Breeze* in there?"

"No, ma'am."

"Good. Sir," she said as she turned to the barkeep, "if you had stopped to ask Tam what he wanted to drink, like a good bartender would, he would have told you that he likes milk. He cannot get drunk and tear up your bar because he never drinks alcohol. On the other hand, if you truly threatened to seriously harm him, or one of his crewmates, he could easily tear you, your staff, and your bar completely to pieces. And if you ever treat anyone from my crew that way again, I might just let him. Do we understand each other?"

"Lady, I don't know who you are, but…"

"Didn't you hear these men calling me 'Captain?' I'm the captain of the *Matagorda Breeze*, and I'll be making a report to the Harbormaster about you and your staff's behavior. No one from my ship will ever set foot in your establishment, and I'll recommend the same to the other Company captains."

"But without the Company sailors, my business will fail!"

"You should have thought of that before you were rude to one of my sailors, then. Good day, Sir." She turned her back on the man and led Adamo and Tam away from the bar. "Come on, men, let's go find us a drink, shall we?" Tam, still shaking, offered his elbow to his captain, which she took, while Adamo walked on her other side.

XXV

PORT OF NEW ORLEANS

A shipping Captain's job can rarely be called boring, but it can often be uneventful. For several months after the night of the storm, the crew fell into a routine. Jerry and Ruby kept in touch, spending time together whenever they could. Gus Ledoux had struck up a courtship with Emma Whitaker in New Orleans, taking the young Harbormaster out for dinner or beignets every time they were in town.

They'd arrived in New Orleans the day before, loaded with barrels of salted beef from Brownsville. Having arrived nearly a day early, unloading was delayed for a couple of hours, but the ship was empty, and Ruby was in the Harbormaster's front office, looking at the dispatch board for a new cargo.

The Harbormaster opened the door to her office. "Ruby, you're here. Come into my office, please."

She followed the woman into her office, closing the door behind her. "What can I do for you?" she asked.

"We have a shipment for you, of a somewhat sensitive nature. The orders came in from Commodore Marquez that you were to be offered this job. You're available, you're reliable, and you're fast, and to top it off, no other ship is available."

"I appreciate the Commodore's confidence in my crew, I'm sure. What's the cargo?"

"A crate of gold bullion. Gold bars, headed to Galveston. You'll be met at the docks by armed men with a passcode that I will give you tomorrow morning, to take your cargo on to its destination, which you have no need to know."

"I understand, Emma. When will we load?"

"Tomorrow morning, the cargo will be brought here, and you will load and leave with the mid-morning tide. Guards will be posted, and no one goes on or off after the crate is loaded, so get your resupply done today. That shipment must arrive day after tomorrow, come hell or high water."

"We can do it. If I may, then, I'm going to go talk to my officers and get us resupplied."

Whitaker said, "Not a word about your cargo to your crew until you've cast off. I don't want any bandits getting an idea to waylay you. Dismissed, Captain. I'll be with the men bringing the cargo at 0830 tomorrow."

"Very good, Harbormaster."

On her way out the door, she looked again at the crumpled message form in her hand:

FROM: Mississippi Mud, Pensacola, FL
TO: Capt, Matagorda Breeze, any port of call
DATE: 11 Oct 2219

Next stop Galveston. Should arrive 15 Oct noon. Hope to see you and your team there. Miss you.
Capt. Jerry

She'd been looking at the dispatch board for anything headed toward Galveston. And the bosses had handed her a prize on a silver platter. She hurried to the telegraph shack to send a message of her own. It seemed unlikely that he'd get it unless he had a stop or passed a signal mast somewhere along the way, but she hoped he would. Thinking things over, it was possible he'd pass close enough for semaphore signals from Mobile sometime late that evening or early the next day if he was making good time.

FROM: Matagorda Breeze, New Orleans, LA
TO: Capt, Mississippi Mud, any port of call
Date: 12 Oct 2219

We are headed for Galveston, ETA 14 Oct late afternoon. Should still be there when you arrive. Need shore leave. Miss you much.
Capt. Ruby

A half-hour later, she and her officers were in her cabin, having been updated on the news. "Colin," she said, "I'm going to assume that there are people on both ends of this run who know, besides the Harbormaster and Commodore Marquez. Do you think, maybe, this might be a tempting enough target to our pirates? They've not been seen by anyone in over a month."

"If it's not, Captain, then we'll never have one. What do you plan to do?"

She looked over the charts just outside the river's entrance. "If we sail mid-morning, then we'll be coming out of the Mouth pretty close to sundown. Let's see if we can find a hidey-hole somewhere in the West Bay. That's what they'll expect us to do. We'll lay low for a few hours, but maybe not pick the best spot to sit it out. And we'll keep watches, as usual, so we've got plenty of men awake and can spot them. The moon isn't full, so visibility will be so-so, but if we put Adamo in the crow's nest, he'll see them. A little before dawn, we'll slip out of there, with everyone awake with their cutlasses close at hand. I'm betting that's when they'll strike if they haven't spotted us overnight."

"It's bold, Captain. When are you going to tell the crew?" Second Mate Clary asked.

"After we drop off our riverman, no way around that, Tom. Otherwise, we won't know if the pirates are the ones that are working with an inside person or not." Clary nodded.

"So, get us resupplied this afternoon, and get everyone back here by midnight. All-hands for breakfast and loading at the usual hour for morning loads."

"Aye, Captain," the men chorused and left her cabin.

I hope we're ready for this, she thought to herself.

Midafternoon the next day, they were sailing down the river, a riverman still aboard. As they approached Pilottown, the man asked her to signal them for pickup, which she ordered. Once the man was off her ship and they'd made it around the next bend in the river, she called for all hands on deck.

"Okay, men, it's just us now. And now I can tell you about this secret crate we took aboard this morning." She told them about their cargo and that she expected trouble with pirates at some point in their journey. "As near as I can figure it, someone in Galveston has been tipping off the pirates, someone who has access to the dispatch board there. It might be someone in New Orleans, but that wouldn't account for all the incidents I know about, as some of those came from other places headed toward Galveston. Plus, most of the incidents we know about happened before Emma Whitaker was in New Orleans. So keep your cutlasses close at hand, gentlemen. I expect a battle sometime tonight or early in the morning."

"The Second's team will take the overnight watch from 0200 to 0700, and half of the First's team, and half of mine, will stay awake and below decks, armed and ready in case of trouble. At 0500, it's all hands awake then, so nap when you can. If they're true to their pattern, they'll strike overnight or early in the morning, possibly just at 0700, when we're switching watches. We'll stagger things so that there are no more than three men on deck at any time, and they'll think they can take us. If we spot 'em, rather than shouting down from the crow's nest, pass it down quietly. We'll pretend not to see them, and let them get close, and then we'll start to run, but leave the jib and topsails just a little loose, let 'em catch us. Then as soon as they grapple, everyone comes out, and we take them."

"Let's try to take some of the devils alive. If they won't surrender, knock 'em out, do what you have to take the fight out of 'em. I'm hoping any we can catch alive can be persuaded to give us some information."

"Everyone clear?" A chorus of "Aye, Cap'n" came up from the deck. "Men, I don't have to tell you this is dangerous. But you all know how to fight, and now's our chance to make things better for everyone."

XXVI

WEST BAY, LOUISIANA

A soft knocking on Ruby's cabin door woke her. "Captain?" she heard Robert Jones' voice.

"Yes, Mr. Jones?"

"Ramirez thinks he's spotted something. The Second Mate asked me to wake everyone up nice and quiet-like and make sure everyone's ready."

"Thank you, Robert. Go wake the rest of the crew. How many are on deck right now?"

"Just Mr. Clary, Ramirez, and Bell."

"Okay. Keep everyone else below. I'll go join them."

"Aye, Captain."

Ruby rolled out of bed, already dressed, and clipped her knives on her belt. Making sure no light was on near the steps up to the deck, she quietly slipped onto the deck. "Any news, Mr. Clary?" she whispered to her Second.

"Captain, Ramirez thought he had them spotted about ten minutes ago, then sighted them again about two minutes ago. He's got 'em. He's pretty sure. They're about a half-mile away, three points off the bow to starboard, moving slow."

"We should be hearing them in a few minutes, then, water against the hull or something. Let's get Adamo down here where he'll be some use."

"Aye, Captain." He turned to Bell and whispered instructions. The rangy man went to the mast and started up. In about a minute, he and Ramirez both scampered down the ropes to the deck.

All four sailors stood still for a moment and heard the soft lapping of water against a surface. Ruby looked to starboard, shielding her eyes against the moonlight, and made out the ghostly shape, not more than 300 yards away.

"Tom, rather than run and let 'em run us down, we take 'em here. Don't try too hard to see 'em. I'll go to the bow with Adamo and Lew, and we'll yell when they grapple."

"Aye, Captain. Jones should have everyone just waiting below by now."

Ducking down, Ruby signaled the two sailors to stay low and go toward the bow, to wait. She peeked through one of the hawse-holes and saw the black shape of the ship moving closer. Silently, she drew her knives and backed away from the gunwale a bit, in case a grappling hook came at them right at that point.

Off in the dark, she heard a man mutter, "One… Two… Three!" and seconds later, a heavy steel hook sailed over the gunwale a few feet forward from Ruby and held fast. She held up her hand and waited until the other boat was alongside, and the first two men had jumped aboard when she yelled "NOW!"

There was a roar from below decks, as her crew boiled up out of the hatch, cutlasses drawn. The pirates who were already on the deck looked suddenly shocked and then found themselves immediately on the defensive, having been rushed by Lew Bell. Two more men were already mid-jump and ended up in the fray in moments. Adamo Ramirez raced past the fighting men and threw a grappling hook of their own into the pirates' vessel, while Tom Clary threw another one at the stern of the vessel, attempting to get a second hook so they could not escape.

Tam roared onto the deck with his shipmates and quickly found his way to his captain's side. They'd never managed to get Tam comfortable with a sword; he preferred his bare fists. But even an armed man didn't have a lot of opportunities to harm the big man; he was amazingly fast for his size, and one blow from his meaty fists could knock men unconscious.

He saw Ruby engaged with the first man who'd landed on the deck, a big fellow with a heavy cutlass. "TAM HELPS THE CAPTAIN," he yelled, as Ruby had the bigger man's sword trapped between her knives. He was applying pressure, and Ruby was leaned over backward under the onslaught. The pirate was so focused on his task that he did not see Tam's fist coming directly at his head. On contact, he reeled to the right, off-balance, and ran shoulder-first into the foremast, going down in a heap.

The fight was over in a moment. The four men on deck were down, two dead, one unconscious, and one, seeing the crowd of angry men coming at him from below, had wisely dropped his sword. Colin had him on his knees, his cutlass at the man's throat as one of the sailors bound his hands behind him with a piece of rope.

Ruby looked around, and seeing no one else to fight, sheathed her knives and took Tam's arm. The big man was breathing heavily, a wild look on his face. "Tam! The fight is over, Tam. Good job!"

"Tam did good?"

"Tam did wonderfully! Good job, Tam. Adamo, why don't you and Tam go below and get him a big mug of milk to help calm him down some."

"Aye, Captain."

Colin sauntered up. "Captain, I know there's at least one more on that ship; I've seen someone peeking up from below."

"Take six men and secure that ship, Colin."

"Aye, ma'am." He waved at the six men nearest him, and they all jumped onto the pirate vessel's deck. In moments, they heard the sound of a scuffle.

"Bosun!"

"Cap'n?"

"Injury report."

"I've laid eyes on everyone on our side of the rail, and no one's down. Two of them are dead, plus that one that Tam flung into the foremast won't wake up for a bit yet. I've got a man securing him now."

"Thank you."

Colin's head popped up out of the stairs of the other vessel. "Captain? Two of them dead, one captured. One injury on our side, Jones got a little scrape. The ship is secure."

"Outstanding. Bring your prisoner over here with these two."

Minutes later, the four bodies were searched for clues as to their identities, and the three prisoners were together by the portside rail. The two conscious prisoners glared grumpily at their captors, and Ruby knelt in front of them.

"Okay, gentlemen, it's time for you to start talking. I need to know where your other crews are, where your hideout is, and who's running this outfit. Which one of you is in charge?"

The smaller man nodded at the unconscious sailor. "He's the boss."

"That so? Well, we'll be chatting shortly. But I want some information from you both, as well."

The larger of the two spat at Ruby. She took a handkerchief from her pocket, calmly wiped her face, then abruptly drew back her arm and slapped the man firmly across the face. "Don't do that again, or I'll have Tam slap you. You're both in a world of trouble, and the only thing that can save you is if you start talking about where your hideout is and how many pirates are in your gang."

"Not telling you nothin', lady."

"Very well, then. Bosun, take these three men and lock them in the number-three hold. Post guards, no one in or out without my permission."

"Aye, Cap'n." Signaling some of the men to help, they hustled the pirates below. Ruby turned and looked at the captured vessel. She was a sloop, single-masted with a fore-and-aft sail, rigged for a jib on the front, about 40 feet long. Clearly, she was built for speed and not for comfort or large capacity.

"Colin, any idea where that hull might have come from?"

"No, ma'am. The Company has a few sloops like that for short runs, but I don't recognize her."

"Maybe we'll find something aboard. Logbooks or something. Whatever you find, send over to me before we take her in; there might be some clues."

Seeing her Second coming down from the quarterdeck, she asked him, "Tom, how much of a prize crew will you need to sail her home with us?"

"Oh, I figure that four men and I can take 'er in if we stick close to you."

"Sounds like a plan. Choose four men—you can't have Ramirez or the bosun. Probably oughta keep Tam in familiar places, too."

"I agree."

"I see no reason to stick around here; let's bring this cargo in, and see who in Galveston comes out with steam coming out of their ears. Let's scram."

Twenty minutes later, the crew of the *Breeze* was getting under way, the smaller vessel following behind and to port. The pirate ship had a shelf for signal flags, but there weren't any flags aboard, so they were keeping close so they could yell or wave back and forth if they needed to.

"Mr. Ramirez! When you get back up in the crow's nest, take a broom with you, and tie it to the mast, right at the top."

"Aye-aye, Captain!"

Shortly after dawn, one of the men from below came to see Ruby on the quarterdeck. "Captain, it sounds like all three prisoners are awake, and one of them is yelling and begging to speak to you."

"Toss 'em into pitch darkness, and one would surely get a little antsy. Take two men, and bring him to me."

"Aye, Captain."

In minutes, the sailor that she'd been fighting, the one the others had fingered as the boss, was brought on deck, held closely by Jones and Tam.

"You wanted to speak to me, sailor?"

"I dunno what those others told you, but I'm the one that was in charge on that boat."

"Well, good, then you're all agreed on that. So, where are you based out of?"

"Nowhere."

"Come now, Captain, we both know better than that. Surely there's someplace where you and your colleagues link up?"

"Ain't sayin'."

"Okay. Gentlemen, take him back to the hold."

"Wait! Don't put me back in there."

"Anxious in the dark, eh? I don't have the time to ask again, mister. Talk, or enjoy the hold."

"Okay, okay. I figure we're dead men anyway. We tie up to the remains of an old oil rig."

"I kind of figured that. But there are thousands of those out there. Where is it located?"

The man rattled off a longitude and latitude, a place due south of the Mouth about 30 miles.

"Do you move often?"

"We haven't moved but once in two years, no need. With all the ships sticking close to the coast, it's a good hideout."

"Good to know. How many pirates, and who leads them?"

"20 men, not counting my crew, plus some women. Leader's a fat old shit named Conrad."

"Are they gonna move if you don't show back up?"

"Conrad probably won't, the fat slob. He'll stay all comfy with his women and say that old tub we were in probably sank. He's lazy. He might send the other sloop out with a few men to take a look around."

"How many ships does he have?"

"Three. Well, two, now. A three-masted schooner, and another sloop like mine."

"How did you know where we were going to be?"

"Conrad told me to take a crew and come search around. How he knew, I dunno, probably someone from the supply run we'd had the day before from Galveston."

Ah-hah, Ruby thought. *But… that means…*

"You realize that if you give any hint of this to the sheriff, you might be tortured into talking. So keep your lips zipped, or tell me to hang you and your men now."

"Days, lady, you're a cold one! I figure we're dead men, anyway. Best kill us now, then. I'd rather die now than go back in that hold again."

"Mr. Jones, take this man to the galley and gag him. We'll be dealing with these men shortly."

A grim look on his face, the burly sailor led his prisoner away. "Aye-aye, Captain. Come on, you."

XXVII

GULF OF MEXICO

"I can't turn them over to the sheriff, Colin! If I do that, then word will get back to Marquez's office, and we'll lose the trail."

"Right, but hanging them after they surrendered…"

Ruby and her First were in her cabin, trying to decide what to do with the captured pirates.

"They're pirates, Colin. They know the penalty for piracy. It's been the law for almost 200 years, since the chaos after the Day. I don't like the idea of having to kill them, but they're dead men any way you look at it. And keeping our advantage over these pirates depends on making sure none of them talk when they go ashore. We've got the information, and tomorrow, I'll talk to Jerry, see if he'll help us root out their nest."

"You're going to get him wrapped up in this mad scheme, Ruby? I thought you liked him."

"I do, Colin. And I trust him. We were talking over dinner last month, and he's as tired of worrying about pirates as every other captain in the fleet. We've got a shot at putting an end to it in the Gulf."

Colin said, "I get that. I just don't like the idea of having a hanging on board this ship, remembering that Captain Nielson did it to himself."

"I'm not crazy about it either, for the same reason. I want to talk to the crew, and I'm not going to force anyone to stay on deck while we do it if they think it'll upset them. And I'll do it myself. It's all on me, and the log will reflect that."

"That's as good a plan as I can think of, Ruby. Best we get it over with. I'll signal Tom to tie up alongside."

When Ruby gathered her crew and told them what she was going to do, no one decided to stay below. Robert Jones told her "we're with you, Captain. Has to be done, it's the law. 'Preciate you saying we don't have to stick around and watch, but I know you. You haven't said, but I betcha it'll be tough on you to do it. I'll stay up here to support you, ma'am." Nods and murmuring of "aye, yeah" joined him from the rest of the crew.

"Thank you, Mr. Jones. Let's get a barrel and some rope, then. Might as well get it done."

The first of the three pirates, their captain, was brought on deck, and made to stand on an empty water barrel next to the foremast. A rope was tied around the barrel, run through a pulley and up into the rigging where a weight hung free. The rope holding this rig in place came to the pin rail near where Ruby stood, her officers beside her. A second rope, secured to the foremast, was placed around the man's neck. Her crew stood in two lines from the hatch below to the makeshift gallows.

"You have been captured in the act of piracy. Under my authority as Captain of this vessel, you are sentenced to die. Do you have any last words?"

The older man looked over at her and said, "thank you for letting me have my dignity, Captain. Do what you have to." He faced aft, back the way he'd come, and closed his eyes.

Ruby took a deep breath, then drew her knife and slashed the rope holding the weight in the rigging. The weight fell toward the deck, pulling the barrel out from under the pirate. It was over in a moment, his neck broken. Two of her men loosed the rope from the rigging, lowered the body to the deck, and reset the gallows for the next pirate.

In less than an hour, it was over, and all seven pirates' bodies had been bound with a weight around their ankles and thrown overboard. As the last of them sunk below the waves, Ruby said, "These men lived and died on the sea. To the sea, we return their bones. May their souls find safe harbor." Without another word, she walked to the hatch below. As she headed down the steps, she heard Colin dismissing the crew.

XXVIII

PORT OF GALVESTON

As the *Matagorda Breeze* and the pirate sloop came alongside the dock later that afternoon, she could see a group of armed men waiting, with Commodore Marquez standing beside them. Once the crew had lowered the gangplank, she walked down beside the men and looked at the armed men expectantly. One of them stepped forward and leaned down to whisper a series of words in her ear. Nodding, she said, "The passcode is good. My men will have the crate ready to unload momentarily." The armed men nodded and began backing a small cart over for the crate.

She turned to the Commodore. "Commodore Marquez, I've brought the shipment in safely. We were beset by pirates but managed to defeat them. My crew and I have brought you this hull as a prize from the battle."

Marquez looked at her, then out to the sloop, just lowering its own gangplank. "Good work, Turner. Did you lose any men?"

"None, sir. One injury, just a scrape. Fortunately, my lookout happened to spot the pirates in the moonlight and got most of us awake before they arrived. We got the jump on them instead of the other way around."

"Hrmph. Well, we'll figure out what to do with her before long. I'll have her sailed around to the dry docks tomorrow. You and your crew get the next three days of shore leave, if you want, once you get me your report on the action tomorrow morning."

"Aye-aye, Commodore. Will that be all, sir?"

He handed her a message form. "Looks like you and Captain Smith have a dinner arrangement tomorrow night. This came in early this morning. Dismissed, Captain. Congratulations."

"Thank you, sir."

She turned and walked back up the gangplank, and told her first mate, "Once they get that crate off here, post a gangway watch, then everyone else is off-duty; it's been a long day for us all. After I turn in my write-up on this in the morning, we get some time off."

"Aye, Cap'n. Get some rest."

As she headed down the ladder below, she looked at the message form:

FROM: Mississippi Mud, signals via Mobile, AL
TO: Capt, Matagorda Breeze, Galveston, TX
DATE: 14 Oct 2219

Looking forward to seeing you tomorrow afternoon.
Capt. Jerry

"We got spotted by pirates just out of the Mouth. The lookout saw them in time and managed to get enough of us awake to deal with them. We caught them by surprise."

Smith looked worried. "How many were there?"

"Seven. It was over in a flash, and I didn't lose anyone, just one nasty scrape on Bob Jones. I put a prize crew on their little sloop, and we brought her in yesterday. But enough shop talk, Captain."

He smiled down at her, relaxing. "I just worry about you, Ruby. We haven't had many pirate attacks the last year or so, but they're out there, and I do not want to lose you."

"I'm a big girl, Jerry, and my crew and I can take care of ourselves. But I'm glad you care. Now kiss me; I need it."

Some time later, she asked, "can I trust you, Jerry?"

He peered at her curiously. "I don't think there's any question about that."

"But what I'm about to show you is big, Jerry. Really, really big. I need to hear it. Nothing we say leaves this cabin. I love you, and if this gets out, bad things could happen to one or both of us or our crews."

Jerry Smith sat up a little straighter in his chair. "Okay, you have my attention. You can trust me."

She relaxed. "Okay, then, let me lay this all out for you." She showed him her charts and what she had deduced about the Gulf pirates. "I was looking this over, after we did that chart, and got to looking for deeper patterns. So, you see, it's almost gotta be someone here in Galveston that's tipping them off. This latest load of mine proves it—we were hauling gold bars, and after months of no trouble at all, we weren't ten hours out of port, and they were on us."

"When I got told what our cargo was, we deliberately made it easy to find us, and we waited up for them. We set a trap and managed to catch them in it. Four of the pirates were killed in the fight, but the other three, we captured. One was their skipper."

"Ruby, what did you do to them?"

"The skipper and I had a talk. He knew he was already a dead man, and he did not want me to turn him over to the sheriff. He knew they'd get it out of him, and he wanted to die with some dignity. He told me how many there were, who was running it, and where their hideout is. After the sun was up a bit, we hung the three who'd survived and buried them at sea."

"That must have been hard for you. I'm sorry."

"It was. It was the only thing that made sense, but I didn't have to like it, and I don't. Jerry, I hope you don't hate me for doing that."

"Why would I? Like you said, they were dead men. They knew what they were getting into, and the law has been clear for more than a century. I can't hate you for that; I admire you. I'm not sure I could have done it."

"So, I know where their hideout is, where they tie up their ships together, and that there are only 20 pirates, plus a handful of women. And odds are that a few of them, maybe five or seven of 'em, are going to be out and about for the next couple of days searching for their companions. So they're under strength."

"Surely you're not thinking of taking them on with just your men, Ruby?"

"Well, my men are well-trained; everyone aboard is spending an hour a day training, and I've got a man as a master-at-arms who's taught us all a lot. But I'm sure that, with those odds, it'll be hard for everyone to come away unscathed."

"More like impossible." Jerry got out of his chair, and looked out the open window in the aft of the cabin, toward his own ship.

"Ruby, I don't think you ought to do this alone."

"But…"

"Hear me out. If you happen to get to this little nest, and they're still there, they'll see you coming two or three miles off. Now, they might scatter, or they might not, and if they don't, you're going to have a hell of a battle on your hands, one you might not win. If they scatter, you're not going to get them all, and we're back to the same old business as usual."

"That's a risk I've got to take, Jerry."

"Sure, but you don't have to take it *alone*, is what I'm saying."

She looked up at him. "You mean…"

"Yes. Let's do this together, Ruby. If we slip up on them at night, from two different approaches, we might catch them sleeping and do this with a lot less bloodshed. My men probably aren't as skilled fighters as yours are, but they'll hold their own. If we can find out who's informing them, then we can sail here and crack this wide open."

"I could loan you my master-at-arms, to train your men for a few days, quietly. When is your next trip?"

"We leave Galveston tomorrow, for New Orleans. Quick turnaround there, and supposed to come back here."

"Jerry, if you sail straight and tight, you can get there faster, and that'll free up some time and give us a better window. My gang and I can pick up some cargo here, or in Corpus Christi, and meet you at the Mouth. You sure you want to do this, Jerry?"

"No, but I'm quite sure you're going to, with or without me. So let's coordinate."

"Okay, then…" the two captains set to work crafting their plan.

XXIX

GULF OF MEXICO, SOUTHWEST OF THE MOUTH OF THE MISSISSIPPI RIVER

"Cap'n Ruby! Two ships tied alongside, two points off the port, 'bout two miles. One's got signals up, but I can't make 'em out just yet."

"That'll be the *Mud*, Mr. Ramirez, but I wonder who he's got with him." Jerry had spoken about a captain he trusted, who, if he was available, could help with this venture, and Ruby had assented to him letting them in on the plan.

Within minutes, Ramirez called down from the crow's nest, "Signals! *Mud* is signaling to come alongside to her starboard."

"Very well, Adamo. Gus, make it happen."

"Aye, Captain."

When they came alongside, Jerry jumped over the rails onto the *Breeze*'s deck and headed for the quarterdeck.

"Ruby, I've got us an extra 22 men. I didn't tell their captain everything, just that we had a hint where the pirates were hiding and did they want in on the capture. He took me up on it. Lincoln Palmer can be trusted. I've known him for years. I know it was risky."

"I hope you're right, love. I've known him a good while, and he seems solid. If this plan works, it'll be nice having the extra men to make it happen. How was Lew Bell?"

"That man is amazing with a cutlass, Ruby. We've all learned a lot in just a couple of days. I think Palmer's crew will do okay; I had Bell sparring with them while we were waiting for you."

Lincoln Palmer, Captain of the schooner *Progreso*, stepped over the rails and joined them. "Captain Turner, it's good to see you. When Jerry told me what he was up to, he didn't tell me who. Your reputation is already solid, even for so new a captain. Congratulations on your battle last week."

"Thank you, Captain. Did Jerry tell you where we are headed?"

"No, just that we were meeting the plan's mastermind here. My cargo is light, and my men are rested, though I have not yet told them why we are here."

"Okay, then. Welcome to the team. Now, let's go over the plan. Jerry, what's your cargo like?"

"I told my crew after we left Pilottown. The *Mud* is middlin' heavy, and my ship is bigger than yours, so I'm probably the slowest of the three."

"I agree; I've got cantaloupe and grapefruit again, so I'm pretty light. Here's what we'll do. Captain Palmer…"

"Lincoln, please, Captain."

"Then call me Ruby. Lincoln, as the gulls fly, we're not but an hour's sailing from their location, about ten miles away to the southwest, here." She pointed at the map. "We're lucky that the wind is out of the south. Jerry will sail straight in, as close to the wind as he can. I'll take right flank, and sail 60 degrees to starboard of him for about ten minutes, then tack back and forth toward that spot. Lincoln, you'll be 60 degrees to port, and you and I will flank them somewhat. If we spot each other, use lights to signal, covered, so we don't get seen. Ideally, we'll all get to that spot just about the same time, and they'll all be asleep. Keep your men quiet on deck as we approach, and maybe we'll get the jump on them."

"It's possible they'll have a lookout, and one or more of us will get sighted. So haul butt in there, don't dilly-dally, even if you're a little quicker than the other two ships. Hopefully, they won't have time to split up. We'll see how many ships they have; they should have only one or two. Keep an eye on the one closest to the side you came in on, and if it splits away, chase her down. Keep enough of your men in reserve to be able to do that, and send the rest on the boarding parties. Try to keep as many alive as you can."

"Why's that, Ruby?" Lincoln asked.

Ruby and Jerry looked at each other for a moment. Ruby replied. "I'm hoping one or more of them has information about how they know where to look for us. Someone, somewhere, is telling them when ships pass close, and I aim to find out who."

"Ah! Good, good. I will tell my men to try to capture prisoners."

"So, that's the plan. Any questions, gentlemen? No? Then send Lew Bell back over to me, Jerry, and let's get the bastards. Lincoln, we'll hold up for a few minutes to let you fill your crew in, then we set out together."

XXX

GULF OF MEXICO, 30 MILES SOUTH OF THE MOUTH OF THE MISSISSIPPI

Adamo Ramirez could see the *Mud* off to port and had reported seeing a glimpse of something where the pirates should be, but he wasn't sure yet. She could see the young man searching the darkness above her.

"There are no lights at all, Cap'n," the young man said quietly, looking down from the masthead. "But I think I see three masts, maybe four. Or three masts and part of an oil rig, maybe the one they're tied up to. Give me another minute or two, and I'll know. It looks like *Mississippi Mud* will get there right after us; we're outpacing her by about three lengths, near as I can make out."

"Good work, Adamo. Keep it up." The *Breeze* was tacking quickly back and forth, zig-zagging toward their target almost directly into a light southerly wind. Jerry Smith's ship was heeled over, sailing very close to the wind; one mistake would put his ship in irons. They'd signaled that they had *Progreso* in sight; Lincoln had gone farther upwind and was making good time with his spinnaker, the wind almost at his stern.

"I got 'er, Cap'n Ruby. Four masts, and a shorter something is sticking up out of the water. Two points off to port. Mile and a half out, or a bit less."

"Gus, switch us to port tack. That'll bring us a little closer to the *Mud*, so keep your eyes peeled. Adamo, would you be able to see them from down here?"

"Yes'm, now that I know where to look. I've got 'em."

"Then get on down here. Silence, everyone. Colin, signal *Mississippi Mud*, let 'em know we're coming in closer. It looks like the pirates don't see us coming."

"Aye, Captain." He took out the tiny lantern and flashed its light toward the other ship, shielding it from their target. In a moment, one short flash acknowledged.

As they got closer, Ruby could make out the shapes of the two ships. The larger one, a three-masted schooner a bit larger than her own ship, was tied to the column of an old sea platform, which was not quite vertically sticking out of the water. The smaller vessel was a single-masted sloop right alongside, on the side closer to her. She tugged on Colin's arm, pulling him down to whisper in his ear, "Signal Jerry. His men go after the schooner; we'll clear the sloop then join him. *Progreso* can't be far behind and will hit the schooner from the other side." The mate nodded and flashed his lamp at the other ship.

The next few minutes were tense as she moved around the deck where her entire crew waited. She'd detailed Gus, Tom, and four others to stay aboard, in case someone tried to get away, but quickly filled the rest in on the situation. As they got close, Gus passed the whispered order to reef the sails almost all the way down so that they could just drift in close. She could clearly make out *Mississippi Mud* doing the same thing as they approached the pirate schooner.

Lew Bell and Robert Jones were standing on the *Breeze*'s rail, holding on to the rigging with one hand, their cutlasses drawn. As they drew close to the sloop, the two men jumped together and landed lightly on her deck. One ran forward, and the other aft, to check the upper deck, as Ruby led the boarding party over the rail and directly toward the steps leading into the sloop's small cabin. Tom and Larry secured the *Breeze* to the sloop's side, as Ruby slipped down the steps and across the corridor into the captain's cabin, Tam and Adamo Ramirez right behind her. The pirate in the tiny cabin's bunk groggily looked up to find Ramirez's cutlass pointed at his face. He slowly took his hands out from under the thin sheet that covered him and held them up. Tam had some short pieces of rope draped around his shoulders and used one to tie the man up.

Ruby heard a scuffle behind her as her boarding party found three other men in bunks in the sloop's crowded forward cabin. One had drawn a knife from beside his bunk and was engaged with Eric Thompson. Thompson's longer weapon was a disadvantage in the close quarters, so he backed toward the door. The pirate struck toward Thompson's left side, and when Eric turned sideways, the pirate quickly reversed course and stuck the knife into Thompson's right side, just below the ribs. The sailor collapsed, and the pirate turned to go back into his cabin to help his mates. He had just stepped through the door when he was struck from behind by Ruby, her knife cutting at the backs of his knees. The man fell to the deck, writhing in pain. She called for Ramirez to help secure the men in the forward cabin and to do what they could for Thompson.

Ruby could hear the sounds of a fight and women screaming from the schooner, and seeing that her crew had things in hand with the remaining pirates on the sloop, she charged up onto the deck. "We're clear below!" she yelled to Bell and Jones, and the three ran up the gangplank onto the higher deck of the schooner.

She could see some of the *Mud*'s men engaged up near the bow, while others, along with Colin and some of her own men were near the hatch leading below. Pirates continued to come up on deck from below, so clearly, the element of surprise was no longer an issue. With the narrow hatchway, only one could move through at a time, and they had to defend themselves immediately.

A minute or so of clanging steel and sailors crying out and the pirates were making headway. Two of the *Mud*'s men had fallen. They had backed Ruby and her crewmates away from the hatch below, making it possible for more reinforcements to join them. Just then, she heard a great yell off to one side, as *Progreso* bumped into the side of the schooner, and Palmer and a dozen of his crew leaped over the rails to join the fray.

The tide had turned, and seeing so many other men joining in, a number of the pirates dropped their swords and fell to their knees. An obese pirate had just come up from the hatch, and he screamed, "On your feet! Fight!" but he found himself surrounded, facing Ruby, both of her knives raised and pointed at his throat.

"Captain Conrad, I presume?"

XXXI

GULF OF MEXICO, 30 MILES SOUTH OF THE MOUTH OF THE MISSISSIPPI RIVER

The pirates had been contained, the dead accounted for, and wounds treated. Ruby had gone below with Jerry and Colin at her heels to check the lower decks, and found five terrified, scrawny women hiding in Conrad's cabin. Sheathing her knives, she spoke to the women, to understand their situations. What she heard infuriated her. She had the hapless women taken to her ship and placed in the empty Navigator's cabin, with Larry Nall watching over them and getting them a good meal.

Ruby had lost one crewman, Eric Thompson, and Jerry had lost three of his, including his second mate. Most of the pirates had not given up easily; twelve were dead, four wounded, and four more were captured without injury, including their leader, Captain Conrad.

The three captains met on deck, where Conrad was tied to his own mizzenmast. "So, Captain," Ruby began, "You've got some talking to do, starting with why you were holding those women captive."

"They weren't captives. They came out here voluntarily."

"That's not the way they tell it, interestingly. They all said that one of your crew hired them as a cuddlebug, and then during the night while they were engaged with their client, the ship sailed away from the port, with them still aboard. That's kidnapping and slavery, Conrad, and it's abhorrent and illegal. For that alone, you are a dead man. But let's talk more about how you manage to have income and survive out here at sea, shall we?"

"We wait for ships coming through, and waylay 'em, that's all. We've been keeping our eyes on the Mouth."

"We're thirty miles from the Mouth, Captain, and from your mainmast, the most you'd be able to see is three or four miles. You're not watching the Mouth, are you? Someone is telling you where to find our ships."

"For such a little girl, you sure seem to think you know a lot. Why aren't these men running things?" the pirate spat, looking at Jerry and Lincoln standing nearby.

Ruby drew back her arm, and slapped him, hard. "That's for calling me a 'little girl,' you son of a bitch. Don't do it again."

Lincoln spoke up, "You will get no help from us, Captain. Captain Turner figured out where you were hiding, and led us here to take you. She's an extraordinary woman, and you should fear her, for your life is very much in her hands right now."

Conrad spat blood, and asked, "How did you find us? This was a perfect spot."

"You know, when you took the *Floridian*, I wanted to find you so badly. You and your crew killed good men, and their captain was my friend and mentor. It was a tragedy, and it hurt a great many people. It was a tragedy, until you sent your men after my ship. Then, it got personal."

"I don't know nothin' about you, lady."

"*Matagorda Breeze*? You sent your other sloop looking for me last week. The good news is, your boyos found us, all right. The bad news is, they're all dead now. Their skipper told me where you were. And here we are," Ruby said.

"And here we are. I suppose you're going to kill me, too."

Ruby replied, "Oh, justice will happen, for you and your men here, Conrad. But you're going to tell us some things first."

"Think so?"

"Oh, yes. You'll be singing like a bird, very soon. Not, mind you, that I need that. The letters in your cabin made it really clear to me who's been sending you word. Too bad you won't get to warn him that we're coming for him." The other two captains looked startled. "Gentlemen, shall we retire to Jerry's cabin for this bit of news? It's closest. Colin, keep an eye on this…creature…for us."

"Aye, Captain."

When the three Captains reached Jerry's cabin, she showed him the letter she'd found in Conrad's desk. It was from Conrad's informant ashore, and when they saw the name, they both blanched.

"But… How long has he been doing this?" Jerry asked dumbfounded.

"Years, I imagine. He's been where he is for more than a decade, and would have been able to do it before then, certainly," Ruby answered.

Lincoln said, "So, what do we do about it?"

"It will be useful to find out how he's dropping the messages. It's not like the pirates could just sail up to the Company docks and pick them up. They've gotta be going to the independent docks. But he wouldn't go there, either, so he's leaving the messages somewhere. They might just be a message drop, but they might be able to identify the person dropping the messages. If it's not him doing it, then there's more to this chain that needs to be dealt with."

Both men were nodding. "Lincoln, where were you headed?"

"I'm off to Tampa, then Havana."

"Okay. Gather your crew and head out of here. And for Days' sake, tell them to keep their mouths shut. Hopefully, by the time you get to Tampa, we'll have this wrapped up. Jerry and I are both headed for Galveston."

"Very well, Captain. Ruby, Jerry, it's been a pleasure serving with you this evening."

"Thank you for your help, Lincoln," Jerry said, shaking the man's hand. Lincoln bowed to Ruby, then took his leave.

Jerry turned to Ruby. "So, what are we going to do with his men? We didn't catch them in the act of piracy, there's just a few tons of evidence that they are pirates."

"Right, so we can't hang them. Do you have room for the men? I'll take the captain, and see what we can get out of him about where his message drop is."

"One of his sailors might have been on those runs. I'll see if I can talk them out of that. And when we get to Galveston?"

"Keep 'em below, and keep 'em quiet. We'll compare notes, and see about this message drop, then we go to the Chairman of the Board; he lives nearby."

"Sounds like a plan. Need me to detail a few men to help bring these ships in?"

"Five of yours, five of mine, and let's keep both ships offshore about thirty miles, until we're ready to go get 'em. I can have Tom command that, if you like, since you're down an officer."

"Good plan. Let's get it in gear."

Back out on deck, the crews had gathered. The prize crews were assigned, and the prisoners taken below in both ships, and the *Mississippi Mud* sailed for Galveston, *Matagorda Breeze* a couple of hours behind her, so no one in Galveston would get suspicious.

XXXII

PORT OF GALVESTON

Upon her arrival in Galveston, Ruby went to the *Mississippi Mud* to see if Jerry had learned anything from his prisoners.

In his cabin, she asked, "did they spill anything, Jerry?"

"Unfortunately, no. Do we have enough to go to the Chairman with what we've got?"

"I hope so. The letters, especially, will help our case. Conrad told me they were mailed to a post-box in Galveston, so we don't have any middlemen to worry about. Give me half an hour, and we'll go."

Walking the five bocks west of the Strand to the Chairman's house, Ruby reached out and nervously took Jerry's hand. "What if we're wrong, Jerry? Is it possible that Conrad could paint himself as an independent gone wrong, and get away with this?"

"I don't see how. We've got his confession with four people present, and we'll all corroborate what happened south of the Mouth. Don't worry, love. We've got this."

The Chairman of the Board for many years had been James Simpson. The Simpson family had controlled the Gulf Shipping Company for generations, maintaining it as a closely-held company. The current family patriarch, Simpson, had served for some years as the Company's chief executive but had slowed down in the last couple of years as his wife's health had declined, so had turned over the day-to-day operations to his son, Daniel Simpson.

Jerry and Ruby walked up to the stately home and were met at the door by a butler, who asked them their business. Jerry answered, "We're Captain Jerry Smith and Captain Ruby Turner. We would like to see Mr. Simpson, please. We have urgent information about criminal activity within the Company." The butler looked startled, then asked them to wait. A couple of minutes later, they were shown into a sitting room at the front of the house, where Mr. Simpson sat at a small desk.

The older man rose as they entered, shaking their hands. "Captains, welcome. I don't think I've met either of you before. I have heard of you, of course, Captain Turner, but which ship are you commanding, if I may ask, Captain Smith?"

Jerry replied, "*Mississippi Mud*, sir."

"Ah, yes! Both of your ships have performed very well recently; I've seen the reports. Now, Charles told me the most disturbing thing. What can I do for you, Captains?"

"If I may, sir?" Ruby said, her chart in her hand. Simpson showed them to a table, and she unrolled her chart. "Late last year, when the *Floridian*'s crew was lost to pirates, Captain Smith and I started wondering how the pirates managed to do what they did. I knew Captain Leedsom from my first day with the Company, Sir, and he was an extraordinary captain; it just did not make sense to me that he would have made a mistake that big. Captain Smith and I were both in Progreso at the time, and Harbormaster Correa and his wife were most helpful, as they'd kept the piracy reports going back several years."

"We collected the information, and this is what we found. This chart represents the last seven years of pirate activity in the Gulf. As you can see, most of the activity has been right here along the Louisiana coast, with another cluster in the Bay of Campeche, though none of those events are in the last two years."

"But looking deeper, we discovered that most of the time, when pirates were encountered, the ships were carrying high-value cargo. A ship carrying foodstuffs or mail or other routine cargo was never attacked, though there were occasional sightings, including one in my own ship. That made us both very suspicious that someone, somewhere, was telling the pirates the ship schedules and manifests. That meant someone with access to the dispatch boards, more than likely. But that didn't help us narrow things down, as there are several people at every port who would have that information."

"But then, last week, I was given a high-value cargo that wasn't on the board at all in New Orleans. A limited number of people knew about it here in Galveston, and only the Harbormaster and the telegrapher in New Orleans knew it. We were attacked by pirates that night, but we were ready and killed or captured the entire crew of seven."

"Good work, Captain," Simpson interjected. "Does that account for the new sloop over in the dry docks?"

"Yes, Sir, it does. My crew and I brought her home. Before he was hanged, the pirate captain gave me information about the location of their hideout and the size and leadership of their gang. Captain Smith and I decided to go to their location, 30 miles south of the Mouth of the Mississippi River, to try to take them. Captain Smith engaged the assistance of Captain Lincoln Palmer and his crew aboard the *Progreso*. Last night, we fought a battle with 20 pirates, losing a total of four men among us and capturing their leader, a Captain Conrad, and several of his crew, along with five women he was holding as slaves aboard his command schooner. We sailed through the night to get here."

"Who led this little expedition?"

Ruby answered, "I did, Sir. We knew that telling the Commodore might compromise the possibility of finding out who in the company was leaking information to the pirates, so we didn't tell anyone. For that, I bear full responsibility."

"As may be. So, is that what brings you to me today, Captain Turner?"

"Yes, Sir. In Conrad's cabin, I found these." She handed him the letters she had located from the pirates' informant. The old man reached into his pocket for his pince-nez glasses, setting them on his nose and reading. As he read, the color seemed to drain from his face. He flipped through the letters, seeing the same name and handwriting in them all.

"Captains, I wish to thank you for bringing me this information. You were absolutely right to come straight to me with this. Would you please stay here? My son is in the house, and I'd very much like for him to see this. You may need to repeat your story for him, Captain Turner."

"I'd be happy to, sir."

Daniel Simpson asked Ruby to walk him through everything she had learned, and as he listened, he nodded, following along. When she had finished, he asked, "And what have you done with this Conrad and the other prisoners, and the women, and the two ships he held?"

"Sir, the ships are about 30 miles out to sea, manned by prize crews led by my Second Mate, Tom Clary. I hold Conrad and the women aboard the *Breeze*, and Captain Smith has the remainder of the surviving crew aboard the *Mud*."

"Captains, you've been most thorough here. We have an airtight case against the pirates here in front of us, as well as their… informant. It infuriates me that he has been stealing from the Company for so long and gone undetected. But we can lay many, many sailors' deaths at his feet as well, and for that, he will certainly hang. If we show up with the sheriff, he might slip away. But the three of us could walk right in and apprehend him, and then summon the sheriff."

Jerry spoke up, "I could go get the sheriff's men, and you and Ruby could go to the harbor. She's more than a match for anyone who isn't heavily armed with those knives of hers."

"A sound plan, Captain Smith. Captain Turner, I have a carriage out front, if you wouldn't mind riding with me? We can be there in minutes. Father? If we may?"

The elder Simpson replied, "Certainly, son. Be careful."

Minutes later, Ruby had the point of her knife at the throat of the informant, his hands raised, still seated at his desk.

"What is the meaning of this, Turner?" Commodore Javier Marquez shouted, "How dare you raise your blade to me!"

"Commodore, you are under arrest for aiding and abetting pirates, contributing to many deaths, and for years of larceny and grand theft. Mr. Simpson?"

The Company's CEO stepped around the door frame. "Good work, Captain. Marquez, you're in a world of trouble. For years you've led these captains, and it was you who was selling them out to pirates all along!"

"You've got nothing to prove these accusations, Turner!" Marquez shouted.

"Oh, but she does," Simpson added. "She and Captain Smith brought the whole thing to my father and me this afternoon. She's quite a detective. The letters to Conrad in your handwriting were the real clincher, though. Oh, please keep your seat," he said as Marquez started to shift. "I'd hate for Captain Turner to have to hurt you before the sheriff gets here."

XXXIII

PORT OF GALVESTON

Within days, the pirate gang and Javier Marquez had been found guilty and hanged. Ruby had sailed out to sea to bring in the captured schooner and sloop, and goods found in the hold of the schooner had furthered the evidence against the pirates, as some of the crates had been labeled as having been aboard the *Floridian.*

The five women that Conrad had kept on his ship had been cared for ashore, and the Company had made a large payment to each of them to take care of their needs. Two had been from New Orleans and were given passage back home to be reunited with their families there. Ruby had sent a letter with them to give to Emma Whitaker, asking her to watch out for them and help them adjust back into a free life.

The Chairman and CEO had asked Ruby and Jerry to keep their ships in the harbor for a few days while matters were settled. On the sixth day, a messenger asked the two captains to come to the former Commodore's office, where the CEO had set up temporary shop to keep things going while a new chief of shipping operations was located. Mystified, the two captains made their way to the office.

"Captains Smith and Turner reporting!"

"Ah, welcome, Captains! Please be seated," Daniel Simpson said, indicating two chairs. His father, James, was seated in a third chair nearby, smiling.

"Captains, we have a problem, and I'd like your help solving it," the Chairman said.

"Sir?" Ruby asked, puzzled.

"As you know, Captains, the year before last, the Company decided to have a new ship built, a barqentine of nearly 400 tons, with which we're planning to start trading from the Gulf all around the Atlantic. Construction is almost complete, and she'll be ready for sea trials in the next couple of months. Whoever captains her could be out of touch with the Company for months at a time, so we want someone with initiative, someone who will represent us well in foreign ports and make sound decisions, with the Company's best interests in mind."

"We have a number of captains who could fill that role, of course, but the one that the Board is most interested in seeing leading that ship, frankly, is you, Captain Turner."

Ruby was thunderstruck. "Me, sir?"

"Ruby Turner, you've proved your loyalty to this Company's interest, not just by capturing the pirates and tracking down Javier Marquez's involvement, but in the way you've been handling your ship in the last year. You're our best Captain, by far. But therein lies the problem."

"Sir?"

"The Board was made aware of your relationship with Captain Smith. We do not disapprove," he said, raising his hand as she started to interrupt, "quite the opposite. You and Captain Smith seem to be quite a good team. But there can only be one captain on a ship, even one of this size."

"Sir, if I may," Jerry interrupted, "I would gladly serve under Captain Turner any day, in any capacity she'd have me aboard."

"Do you think you two could serve as Captain and First together?"

Jerry said, "I could, absolutely," as Ruby nodded her head, still numb with the surprise.

"Cat got your tongue, Captain Turner?"

Ruby took a deep breath. "This is quite a surprise, sir. Jerry, are you sure you could take the pay cut just to go with me?"

"I could, love. In a heartbeat."

"Ahem, well," Daniel Simpson interrupted, "you wouldn't have to. All positions on this vessel, because of its' nature, will be one pay grade higher than the same position on the schooners you're on now. You'll get a nice raise, too, Captain."

"But what about my crew?" Ruby asked the CEO. "Those men have had a hard road."

"Captain, since it's a totally new ship, you'd have your pick of the crew. I presume you're going to want to bring most of your current crew with you, plus quite a few, if not all, of Captain Smith's men. You're going to need a total complement of sixty, so you'll have to find a few more to fill up the ranks. We can re-crew the *Breeze* and *Mississippi Mud* in time; there are plenty of up-and-comers we can put to work."

"If that's the case, then I'm honored, sirs. I'm happy to accept. Jerry?"

"Me too. This is an opportunity of a lifetime."

"Well, then, that's settled," the Chairman said, rising from his chair. "Danny, I'll leave this in your capable hands. My wife is waiting for me to take her to dinner." He walked out.

"Thanks, Dad, and give Mother my love. Captains, I'll be cutting orders tomorrow for you both to take command of the *Gulf Stream*, so you can start assembling your crew. You'll retain command of your current ships until she starts sea trials, and we may send you on some runs here and there when we need you, but I want you spending most of your time working with the shipwrights and making sure that *Gulf Stream* is shipshape. Your new crew is going to need to learn square-rigging, but I don't think that'll be a big problem. And there is one other thing I'd like for you to do, Turner."

"What's that, sir?"

"I'd like for you to teach the other captains in the fleet the secret of your success. I started looking at your shipping records, and it seems to me you're probably sailing straight courses rather than hugging the coasts, am I correct?"

"You are, sir."

"Well, then, teaching the other Captains and Navigators will be of value to the Company. We can carry more cargo in less time. We'll handle them as they come through Galveston and get everyone doing that."

"I'm happy to do that, sir. I'd like to also talk with the Captains about better managing their relationship with their crews. That has been an important factor in the success I've had."

"Certainly, anything you want to pass along to the other Captains, you'll have your chance. This is a new era for the Company, Captains, and the two of you are on the ground floor of it. Congratulations. Dismissed."

XXXIV

PORT OF GALVESTON

Larry Nall sat on the balcony of his small second-floor apartment at the Company docks only a couple of blocks away. He had rented the place specifically to sit and watch the sunrise, the activity on the docks, and watch for ships coming and going with old friends aboard.

After Ruby was given command of the *Gulf Stream*, Nall realized that he was feeling his years more and more and that it might be past time for him to retire. At the time of his retirement, he was the oldest sailor in the Company, and older, in fact than anyone working for the organization, including its new young CEO. The reward for bringing down the Gulf piracy ring was enough to set up for the rest of his life, with some careful investments to some up-and-coming local businesses, so it's not like he needed the money.

Some of his crewmates had decided against going on the *Gulf Stream*, as well, including Tom Clary, *Matagorda Breeze*'s Second. Tom had a wife and teenage children in Galveston and felt that he was gone from Galveston more than enough. He'd been given command of the *Mississippi Mud* once Ruby's new ship was afloat, and a handful of her current crew had stayed on, along with a few others from the *Breeze.*

Good men, all of 'em, Larry thought to himself. *Oceangoing isn't for everyone.* When he retired, he thought it wasn't for him, but two months later, when the *Gulf Stream* had been launched and started her sea trials, he was watching, and he got a wistful…something...deep in his soul. It wasn't the adventure of it, really, he chided himself, just something about a comfortable group of people, a purpose, and a home.

Simón Correa had been promoted to the Commodore's post, which Larry found to be a satisfactory solution. He'd always liked Correa as a Harbormaster, and his wife was a wonderful help-meet and assistant to him. When they had arrived in Galveston aboard the *Breeze*, he'd waited a few days to let Correa settle in, then paid him a visit just to welcome him to town. Correa had responded by inviting Nall over to dinner with his family, and they had since become good friends.

The Commodore kept Larry up-to-date on the happenings on the docks, and Larry told the Commodore and his family sea stories of his time on the several ships he'd served with over the years.

One evening after dessert, and after the Correa children had been sent to bed, the Commodore was sitting with Larry on the patio of their home, sipping wine. "Do you ever miss it, old-timer?" Simón asked.

Larry had to think about that for a while. "I don't miss the hard, heavy work, no. And managing the deck is a lot more work for a bosun than a lot of people think; it's a personnel job, a leadership job, as much as it is physical. But there are things I do miss, yes."

"Oh? Like what?"

"Like sunrises over the sea, when it's not too windy. A good pot of black coffee on a damp day when it's raining. The camaraderie. Have you ever been to sea, Simón?"

"Only on my trip here from Progreso. I'm from Merida originally, so I had not strayed far from home."

Larry took a thoughtful sip of his wine. "Home. Interesting word, that. I've never had family to speak of; my only brother died young, and I never married, so everyone I'm related to is gone. I always called Galveston 'home', just because I was based here, but I don't hardly know anyone, 'cept Company folk. I guess home was always a ship, for me."

The Commodore looked at him curiously. "Larry, I cannot fully understand that life, as I have never lived it. But I do know that you do not belong here in Galveston."

Larry chuckled, "I suppose I don't, though how a man not much more than half my age would know that I haven't a clue."

"I see it in your eyes, Larry. When you come to the docks, I see the longing looks you give the ships. Home is a ship for you, just as it always has been. Apropos of nothing whatever, I had an interesting conversation with "La Capitána," as my children call Captain Turner, just the other day."

"Whenever an officer says 'apropos of nothing whatever,' I get nervous. They've usually got some crazy idea up their sleeve," Larry replied.

"Normally, I would agree with you. But Captain Turner and I were discussing a problem she has, and I just thought that I might have a solution for her."

Then the Commodore told him, and Larry's soul cried happily.

XXXV

PORT OF GALVESTON, THE NEXT MORNING

Larry and the Commodore walked down the docks toward the *Gulf Stream*, and when they got to the gangplank, Adamo Ramirez was waiting for them.

"Commodore, it's a pleasure to have you aboard, of course, and Bosun, you know you're welcome on our deck any time. May I help you, gentlemen?"

Correa replied for them both, "Mr. Nall and I would like to speak to your Captain, if you don't mind, Crewman Ramirez."

"She is in her cabin with the officers, Commodore. I'm sure she would not mind if you gentlemen barged in on their meeting."

Going down the steps to the crew deck, they knocked on the door and were answered by the Captain herself. "Commodore, welcome! We were just finishing up a little staff meeting. And Larry, you old treasure! How are the knees?" she said in a rush, hugging Larry fondly.

"May we enter, Captain? I would like to discuss something with you and your officers if you do not mind."

"Of course, Commodore, please, come in. Colin, Jim, can you rustle up a couple of chairs for these gentlemen?"

After chairs and ice-cold lemonade were brought, Ruby sat down at her small desk. "Now, Commodore, how may I help you?"

"You recall, Ruby, that we spoke earlier in the week about your staffing problem in the galley."

"How could I forget? No one wants the job of head-cook for sixty people, on top of their usual deck work. Rotation isn't going to work, either, as we don't have that many good cooks. Most of 'em can avoid burning the bacon, but none have the skill that Larry does, for instance. And that would still leave us in the lurch for someone who can plan a good set of meals and find good deals on supplies and produce when we're in port. It's a way bigger job on this ship than on the schooners."

Larry spoke up for the first time. "Well, Missy…beggin' your pardon, Captain…but the Commodore and I have been talking. I don't belong in Galveston, nor any other dry-foot city, for that matter. I belong on the sea, and the Commodore here figured out what's been eating at me for the last two months. I miss this…just sitting around with you, being on a ship, being part of a family of sailors. But I can't work on deck anymore, really, and I wouldn't wanna unseat Bosun Wheatley here, you've picked a good 'un. But I can still cook, and plan meals, and make up supplies orders, and shop for food, just like I always did."

Ruby's eyes were wide. "Larry, you can do all that?"

"I can, for a few years yet. And the Commodore has suggested that I find some youngster to apprentice to me and give me a hand when I need it, so when I'm gone, the crew won't starve."

"…Commodore?" Ruby asked, a question in her eyes.

"I have spoken to Staffing, and two additional hands aboard is not going to be a problem if you can find bunks for them. Larry will make Bosun's wages, and his apprentice can be a Crewman or Senior Crewman."

"Or woman," Larry chimed in. "I know you've hired two more women aboard, Cap'n."

Ruby looked around the room at her officers. "Any objections or refinements to this plan, gentlemen?" But her team was all smiles and vigorous nods, so she rose to her feet. "Chief Cook Larry Nall, welcome to the team," she said, holding out her hand to the old man, who rose slowly, tears in his eyes.

When he reached out his weathered hand to take hers, she pulled him into a tight hug. "I'm so glad you're here, Larry. I need you by my side with your wisdom and love, not just as a cook."

"You'll have that as long as I live, Ruby."

EPILOGUE

PORT OF GALVESTON, SIX MONTHS LATER

Ruby Turner-Smith woke at first light, sheltered in the arms of her husband and First Mate. He was still asleep; she could feel his breath against her neck.

It had been a busy six months. Colin Sampson had served as Second Mate, and Jerry's former First and Navigator were aboard as Supercargo and Navigator, respectively. Jim Wheatley, Jerry's bosun, had taken the same billet on the *Gulf Stream*. Most of the men on both crews had come with them, and they'd added others to fill out a total ship's company of 60.

Tom Clary had declined to come. He had family in Galveston and wished to stay close. He was given command of the *Mississippi Mud*, and the remaining men who stayed behind from both crews joined him. Gus Ledoux had also declined to come along and transferred to a shore job in New Orleans to spend more time with his family and pursue his growing relationship with Emma Whitaker.

Simón Correa was the new Commodore, and Ruby and her team had been privileged to sail the *Breeze* to Progreso to bring him and his family to Galveston to take his new job. The two Correa daughters, 6 and 9, had been thrilled to get to go to sea and held Ruby up as an idol, insisting to their father that they would be great sailors like "La Capitána" when they grew up.

The two girls had been fascinated by Tam, and the gentle man had let them follow him around on deck during the trip, during his off-hours, sat on a corner of the deck with them playing with a balero, the cup-and-ball game. The toy looked tiny in Tam's huge hands, but Tam quickly got very good with the game after being given some time to experiment. When the ship arrived in Galveston, the girls gave it to him to remember them, saying that their father would get them a new one. The giant man dropped to one knee at the foot of the gangplank to hug the girls, happy tears in his eyes, when they departed.

During their first overnight sea trial, their first night out as a crew, the whole crew was on deck having dinner under the open sky. Larry had made an excellent dinner of enchiladas and Mexican corn, with his young apprentice's help, a young woman of 19 named Mary. "She's got some good recipes and is a dandy cook for a small dinner, Cap'n. I'll raise her up right," Larry said when he'd introduced the woman to her new Captain.

After dessert, Jerry stood up, clanked his mug against the railing to get attention, and said, "It's our first night as a crew together, so this seems like a good time to do something I've wanted to do for months now," turned and got down on one knee and said to Ruby, "Captain Ruby Turner, will you be my wife?" Of course, she had said yes, and the wedding was held on the deck of the *Gulf Stream* with the whole crew and many friends present.

Ruby carefully rolled over in Jerry's arms, kissing him gently. "Sweetheart, we need to get up. The high tide is in four hours. You don't want to be late on our maiden voyage."

"Mmf. Okay, I think I'm awake."

After dressing, the couple walked down the corridor to the ship's mess, where most of the crew was gathered. Colin Sampson saw them coming in and yelled, "Captain on deck!" The whole crew bolted to their feet.

"As you were, men. It's a big day today. Enjoy your breakfast."

Two hours later, as the *Gulf Stream* left Galveston Harbor on her first trading voyage, ships all around the harbor were flying signals congratulating them and wishing them well. Dockworkers lined the docks, cheering. Ruby stood on the quarterdeck, her husband at the helm. Her crew lined the rails, waving and cheering.

"Captain, final signals from the Harbormaster. '*Gulf Stream*, best wishes for a successful maiden voyage. Come back with all flags flying. Fair winds to you. Tell Tam the girls said hello, and to please be safe.'"

Ruby smiled at the message's contents and raised the acknowledgment signal herself.

"Captain, we've cleared the harbor markers. Your orders?" Jerry asked.

"First, turn us north to make the Bolivar notch, then we're off. Next stop, New York."

"Aye-aye, Captain! New York, here we come!"

About the Author

Lyla Hopper describes herself as "no one of consequence, just a wife, writer, public speaker, software developer, and full-time RVer." Sh e and her husband and their dog travel around the United States enjoying beautiful scenery and meeting friendly people. Lyla spent her high-school years in East Texas, the home of many wonderful lakes, moving there when her father retired to "go fishing every day until the day I die." *Matagorda Breeze* is her first novel.

Made in the USA
Coppell, TX
28 January 2021

49046593R00108